HIGHLAND DEVOTION
The Band of Cousins, Book 7
Copyright © 2019 by Keira Montclair

Printed in the USA.

Cover Design and Interior Format

© THE KILLION GROUP, INC.

HIGHLAND DEVOTION

7 THE BAND OF COUSINS

KEIRA MONTCLAIR

NOVELS BY KEIRA MONTCLAIR

THE BAND OF COUSINS
HIGHLAND VENGEANCE
HIGHLAND ABDUCTION
HIGHLAND RETRIBUTION
HIGHLAND LIES
HIGHLAND FORTITUDE
HIGHLAND RESILIENCE
HIGHLAND DEVOTION
HIGHLAND BRAWN-COMING SOON

THE CLAN GRANT SERIES
#1-RESCUED BY A HIGHLANDER-
Alex and Maddie
#2-HEALING A HIGHLANDER'S HEART-
Brenna and Quade
#3-LOVE LETTERS FROM LARGS-
Brodie and Celestina
#4-JOURNEY TO THE HIGHLANDS-
Robbie and Caralyn
#5-HIGHLAND SPARKS-
Logan and Gwyneth
#6-MY DESPERATE HIGHLANDER-
Micheil and Diana
#7-THE BRIGHTEST STAR IN THE HIGHLANDS -
Jennie and Aedan
#8- HIGHLAND HARMONY-
Avelina and Drew

THE GRANTS AND RAMSAYS

FAMILY TREE (1280s)

———

GRANTS

LAIRD ALEXANDER GRANT and wife, MADDIE
John (Jake) and wife, Aline
James (Jamie) and wife, Gracie
Kyla and husband, Finlay
Connor
Elizabeth
Maeve (adopted)

BRENNA GRANT and husband, QUADE RAMSAY
Torrian (Quade's son from his first marriage) and wife, Heather—daughter, Nellie (Heather's daughter from a previous relationship) and son, Lachlan
Lily (Quade's daughter from his first marriage) and husband, Kyle—twin daughters, Lise and Liliana
Bethia and husband, Donnan—son, Drystan
Gregor
Jennet
Geva (adopted)
Emma (adopted)

ROBBIE GRANT and wife, CARALYN
Ashlyn (Caralyn's daughter from a previous relationship)

and husband, Magnus—daughter, Ishbel
Gracie (Caralyn's daughter from a previous relationship)
and husband, Jamie
Rodric (Roddy) and wife, Rose
Padraig

BRODIE GRANT and wife, CELESTINA
Loki (adopted) and wife, Arabella—sons, Kenzie
(adopted) and Lucas, daughter, Ami (adopted)
Braden and wife, Cairstine—son, Steenie (Cairstine's son
from previous relationship)
Catriona
Alison

**JENNIE GRANT and husband, AEDAN
CAMERON**
Riley
Tara
Brin

RAMSAYS

—

**QUADE RAMSAY and wife, BRENNA GRANT
(see Grant Tree)**

LOGAN RAMSAY and wife, GWYNETH
Molly (adopted) and husband, Tormod
Maggie (adopted) and husband, Will
Sorcha and husband, Cailean
Gavin and wife, Merewen
Brigid
Simone (adopted)
Beatris (adopted)

MICHEIL RAMSAY and wife, DIANA
David and wife, Anna
Daniel and wife, Constance
Crisly (adopted)
Mariana (adopted)

AVELINA RAMSAY and DREW MENZIE
Elyse
Tad
Tomag
Maitland

CHAPTER ONE

L INET BAIRD PULLED HER MANTLE closer against the biting wind of the Scottish Highlands. Inverness was much colder than her home had been. She'd just come from an inn outside of the royal burgh, the place where she'd hoped to see her sister one last time. Merewen had not been there, so she'd had no choice but to leave her package with a note attached.

She'd likely never see her only sister, her beloved Winnie, ever again.

The thought filled her with despair, but she'd made her choice and intended to see it through. She was needed here, and for something other than serving men.

Living with her family at Clan Ramsay, she'd been at the mercy of her two brothers and her sire, who'd never once thanked her for cleaning their clothes and cooking their meals. They'd only ever asked for more.

And then there was the other purpose she had served for a certain man. She cringed and forced the horrible memory from her mind.

At least she'd escaped him.

She had almost reached the building she slept in with Sela, her boss of sorts, when a strange metallic sound reached her ears, causing her to stop dead in her tracks. The noise grew louder. There were distant yells, too. Pained cries. The area was nearly deserted, except for the two guards with her, so she climbed a small hill to get a better vantage point. The men followed her.

The three of them froze at the top of the hill, shocked by the sight in front of them. Not far from the shore of the River Ness, a battle took place between men guarding multiple crates and a group of Highlanders, some in their tunics and tartans, others dressed in all black. Arrows sluiced through the air, taking men out in seconds. While some fought on foot, others fought on horseback.

Having spent most of her life protected by the warriors and reputation of Clan Ramsay, she'd never witnessed anything so gruesome.

"What's happening?" she whispered, though she knew better than to expect an answer. The guards never addressed her.

"Saints preserve us, but the Highland savages have gone daft." The man to her right stared down at the unfolding chaos, the cacophony doing what nothing else could. He had finally spoken to her.

A frightened screech came from behind her, and when she whirled around to see who had made the grating sound, she was shocked to see Sela in the doorway of the inn. The beautiful woman was not in her usual flowing gown and regal mantle, but a wool gown with trews underneath, her long white-blonde hair falling loosely over her shoulders. Even in such plain clothing, she had an elegance that could not be taken from her—and it did not take her long to regain her usual composure. "Get your things, Leena," she said, using her assumed name for Linet. "I have strict instructions that we're to leave at once with three others. We will travel with ten guards. The rest will follow." Sela was in charge of all the lasses, which afforded her rights and luxuries the others didn't have, but Linet suspected she still wasn't free. She had her orders, just like the rest of them did.

Linet's heart raced as fear crawled up the back of her neck, but she did her best to quell the urge to cry and shriek and run, the thought of being impaled by a sword foremost in her mind. "Are you certain the warriors down there are after us? Some of those are Ramsay and Grant plaids. They'll not hurt us."

"Like hell," muttered one of her guards, shoving her toward the building. "They're all bloody savages. Now go. Some are coming this way."

Her eyes darted back to the battle. The violence made her gasp, but before she could turn away, someone caught her eye. She shouldn't have seen him at all—he was perched in a tree, nearly out of sight—except she was used to stealing glances at this particular man.

Gregor Ramsay.

Her heart squeezed at the thought of him being hurt, though he was in a tree firing arrows at men with a deadly aim. Gregor had given her the best gift of all—he'd taught her to read, which had expanded her world beyond the trap of her parents' cottage. And because he was so kind and handsome, so smart and noble and funny, she'd dared to hope that perhaps their friendship could lead some-where.

The heady dreams of a foolish girl. Her brothers, who'd noticed her interest in the chieftain's son, had been quick to remind her that noble lads married noble lasses, not someone like Linet Baird who spent her days washing clothing in the burn and cooking stew.

And then there was that other reason why someone like Gregor would never marry her...

"Leena, come! *Now!*" Sela's threat did not fall on deaf ears. While she wished to stay and make sure her fellow clansmen fared well, she didn't dare cross the cold Norse-woman known to others as the Ice Queen.

With one glance back, Linet hurried into the building. It only took her a minute to clear the room she'd lived in for the last several days.

Sela waited for her in the hall, her expression tight. "We

leave now. We must get ahead of them."

"Where is everyone? Where are all the other lasses?" Her job was to care for Sela's lasses, was it not? How could she do that if most of them were gone? She'd treated at least twenty lasses since Sela had given her the job of tending to the others' injuries. There could be many more.

"Some have left, some have been given different assignments. It does not matter, but we must leave now." Sela grabbed her hand and tugged her toward the door.

Linet did as she was told, not asking any more questions because Sela did not like to be questioned. Her only alternative would be to stay behind, in which case she'd be forced to travel back with Clan Ramsay.

Never.

True, Sela could be harsh, but she was generally kind to Linet. Everyone knew that. For now, she would do as she was told. It suited her, since she would just as soon be far, far away from whatever was happening on shore. She only hoped Merewen was safe. Privately, she also hoped that the Ramsays and Grants came out ahead.

She greeted her horse once she'd tied her things to the saddle, then waited for assistance in mounting. When one of the guards came close enough to lift her, he whispered, "Many of the lasses have been sent away and not to a pretty place. Be grateful you're not one of them, probably your healer skills have saved your skin. Ask no questions and go."

"But where are we going?" she whispered, her gaze searching his.

"Edinburgh. I pray we make it out."

At least they weren't headed to Ramsay land.

She could never go back home.

———◆———

Gregor Ramsay rolled over, cursing the bumps in the ground where he lay, attempting to sleep but failing miserably. How many times had he made this voyage between

Clan Grant and Clan Ramsay? How many times had he slept in the wilderness of the Highlands? Usually, it took him seconds to fall asleep, but the sounds of the forest affected him differently of late, sending a chill up his backbone.

Reivers he could handle. It was the notorious men in the Channel of Dubh who had his guard up. After the heartlessness they'd witnessed in Inverness, he just couldn't sleep well. Although they'd seen the Channel's cruelty on several occasions, this time they'd unpacked the lasses out of the crates they'd been stowed in for the journey across the sea. His heart had quailed at the sight of those sleeping lasses, drugged and treated like cargo. Bought and sold. At least they'd given the bastards a good dance on their way out of Inverness. They'd killed many of them, though some had escaped.

This was why the Band of Cousins' work was so important. They needed to stomp out what remained of the network.

But his thoughts kept snagging on Linet Baird. Lovely Linet. Although they'd come to Inverness in the hopes of finding her, she'd refused to come home with them, choosing instead to stay with Sela, the woman who'd supposedly run the burgh's underground fighting rings and whorehouses. All of the coin had gone to Sela or her bosses, of course, not the lasses themselves.

Sela had fled during the battle, and Linet had disappeared with her. He suspected that she was not truly in control of the Channel activities in Inverness, but even if she was following orders, she likely had useful information. Perhaps she even knew who led the Channel as a whole.

Sela's level of involvement didn't matter. He didn't like the thought of her having control of Linet. Although he didn't understand what drove Linet, or why she'd refused to come home, he had vowed to find out.

He had vowed to protect her and he would not let up.

They'd spent quite a bit of time together when they were younger. He'd spent the better part of a summer teaching her to read. Whenever he thought of her, he thought of her sweet smile, her distracting lavender scent, and her quick mind. One of his favorite memories of the time they'd spent together was the way her tongue would work its way between her lips whenever she was concentrating, something that had invariably made him smile. Her response was always the same. "What is it?" she'd ask.

"Just you," he'd say. If pushed for more of an answer, he'd say he was impressed with how hard she worked, which was true. He'd concealed the rest of the truth—that the sight of her wee tongue had made him wish to capture it in his mouth.

To say such a thing would have been bold, and at the time he'd been anything but.

Gregor had hoped things might change between them with time, but he'd hesitated to declare himself, and then his duties with the Band of Cousins had kept him away from home. Now she was gone. Missing. This wasn't how he'd imagined they would be reunited.

Connor wanted to help him follow her, fortunately. They had agreed to make quick stops at both Grant Castle and Ramsay Castle on their way to Edinburgh. Once they reached their destination, they suspected they would find Sela and what remained of the Channel. Will and Maggie, the leaders of the Band of Cousins, had stayed in Inverness to search it more thoroughly, but they intended to join them as soon as possible. Merewen and Gavin traveled with them to Grant land. After the healers at Clan Grant treated Merewen's wounds, something that could take a day or two, the new couple would travel to Ramsay land and spend a day or two there before rejoining the Band's mission.

Connor and Gregor would not wait.

A brushing sound perked Gregor's ears, snapping him

out of his thoughts. He sat up, scanning the area for reivers or beasts. His cousins were asleep. Connor Grant lightly snored next to him while Gavin and his new wife, Merewen, lay not far away, snuggling in the cold.

His gut told him something was out there. But what? He grabbed his bow and his quiver, stepping past his cousins and moving farther away from the Ramsay guards stationed a short distance from their small group.

A faint whisper called out to him. "Gregor, is something out there?"

Connor's voice. Before he could reply, a twig snapped not far from him.

Two seconds later, two men came straight at Gregor, swords lifted and aimed to kill.

Hellfire, but this was another one of those times where Gregor wished he'd worked harder at developing his sword skills. His sword lay useless on the ground beside the spot he'd left, a mistake a more proficient swordsman would never have made. He had two choices, his bow or his measly daggers.

Gregor bellowed a warning to the others—Connor, at least, was awake to hear it—and tossed his bow down, reaching for the dagger inside his boot. Nearly upon him, the bastards bore down, the moonlight bouncing off the blades the men carried.

Two large swords.

Aimed directly at him.

He threw himself on the ground, rolled away, and jumped back to give himself enough range to fire his dagger, which he did, catching one of his attackers in the soft part of his belly. But it wasn't enough to stop him.

Gregor was a dead man. He couldn't get away from them fast enough, and Connor was too far away to come to his assistance.

As he readied the second dagger, flashes of his dear mother and father appeared in his vision. His brother and his sisters. He threw the dagger, wounding the second man, but it only seemed to make him more angry. Both men kept coming—until Connor jumped in front of Gregor and cut down the reivers with a single swing of his sword.

They barely made a sound as they fell to the ground in a heap, dead.

"Hellfire, Gregor," Connor said, panting. "You've got to carry your sword. I know you prefer your bow, but it's useless up close. Those puny daggers aren't going to stop anyone in the middle of a forest." He wiped his sword clean on the clothing of the man on the ground closest to him.

Gavin bolted up from his spot, his sword ready for battle within seconds. A few other guards were fast behind him. Uncle Logan, also known as the Beast of the Highlands, had forced Gavin to work in the lists, so he was skilled in the use of several weapons—swords, bow and arrow, daggers, and fists.

Gregor wiped the sweat off his upper lip, cursing. "Hell, Connor, I'm going to have to improve quickly if I'm to go after Linet. I don't know that I could have cut them both down with my sword the way you did."

"Aye, but you must have some skills. Your brother is a skilled swordsman. Didn't Torrian make you practice?"

Gregor thought back to the times when he'd suffered through the lists, fighting his brother, his cousin, or Cailean MacAdam, now known as one of the best swordsmen in the Ramsay clan. He'd had some skills, but he was an exceptional archer and had always preferred the archery butts to the lists.

Gregor's parents had been of the mind that he needn't rely on a sword if he was good enough with his bow and his dagger, so they had never pushed him. Torrian, on the other hand, had insisted his life could depend on his sword skills someday. Since his brother was rarely so insistent about anything, he'd gone to the lists occasionally, but his heart had never been in it.

He should have listened.

Gregor did his best to calm his rapid breathing, his body still reminding him how close he'd come to death. "We were planning to stop at Ramsay land anyway. I'll train with my sword for a couple of days before we continue on. I cannot leave our protection to you, Connor. My apologies."

Connor tipped his head with a smirk. "Clearly, you're not without valuable skills, Gregor. Without you, they'd have caught us all unaware and cut our throats before we even opened our eyes."

Yawning, Gavin stretched his arms overhead and said, "I'd have heard them before then."

Connor quirked his brow at his newly-wed cousin. "Aye, for certes considering you were asleep with your head buried in your wife's bosom. I'm sure you would have heard them."

Gavin chuckled, a sheepish grin crossing his face. "'Tis my favorite way to sleep. Someday you two will learn. Sweet-smelling and soft."

"Aye, so were your mama's," Connor drawled.

Gavin covered his ears. "Nay, nay, nay. 'Tis completely different. Och, why put that in my head?"

Merewen sat up, brushing the sleep out of her eyes. "Gavin, did you miss something?"

Gregor grinned at his cousins' antics, but he couldn't shake the memory of what had happened—and how much worse it could have been. "Wake up all the guards. Send them out to check the area for more reivers."

Gavin moved over to the guards. "I'll take care of it."

By the time they finished searching the area, the sun was nearly up. Fortunately, Gregor caught a glimpse of a well-protected apple tree inside a group of pines. There were still a few pieces of fruit firm enough to eat, so he picked what he could and brought it back to the group, offering one to Merewen, who accepted with a huge smile.

They didn't need to eat much. They'd be back on Grant land mid-day, and then Gregor and Connor planned to continue on to Ramsay land the next morn.

When they arrived, Gregor had much to do with his brother.

CHAPTER TWO

GREGOR AND CONNOR SAT AT the Grant dais in the great hall that night, a veritable feast in front of them, though Connor's family had received no notice they'd be visiting. Uncle Alex and Aunt Maddie, Connor's parents, ate with them, along with his older brothers, Jake and Jamie. His three sisters were with Gracie at her mother's cottage. Merewen and Gavin had already settled in for the night abovestairs.

By the time they finished their account of all that had taken place in Inverness, the food had gone cold on everyone's plates.

"You think there are more men in the Channel?" Jake asked, setting his goblet down and pushing his chair back from the table. "Is this a never-ending saga of torture or what?"

Connor said, "Nay, I believe we're close. Maggie and Will said the men in charge of the organization are English. We'll see what we can find in Edinburgh, then, if need be, finish in England. If we can stop the leaders, we're hopeful we can put an end to the Channel for good. Besides—" he added, casting a glance at Gregor, "—we're trying to help Linet Baird."

Gregor nodded. "I believe Linet's being forced into some kind of servitude. I intend to get her away from it, even though she told her sister she wishes to stay with her companions."

Uncle Alex, one of the wisest men in the Highlands, looked at his youngest son and asked, "And what is your other reason for traveling with Gregor?"

Aunt Maddie said, "I think 'tis obvious, Alex. He wishes to put an end to this before these villains come to Grant land. They took poor Linet from her bed. What will stop them from trying the same thing here?"

Uncle Alex leaned over and kissed his wife's cheek, lingering a bit. "You have a valid point, sweeting, but I'd like to hear our son's answer."

Connor cleared his throat, his way of delaying his response. Gregor knew his cousin strived to be like Uncle Alex—although Connor wasn't quite as good at concealing his thoughts and emotions, he was improving.

When Connor spoke, he looked his father in the eye and said, "Another woman is tied up with their organization. Sela, who ran the fighting and whoring in Inverness. She's as cold-hearted as any I've ever met." He paused again, considering his words.

Jamie grinned, his brows waggling. "But she caught your eye, aye, brother?"

Although Jake started grinning, too, he said nothing but waited to hear what Connor would say.

"And why would you go after a woman who has no respect for other women?" Uncle Alex asked.

Connor didn't hesitate this time, his quick response as telling as the words he chose. "Because I think she's being used, and I'd like to know why." He glanced at his mother. "At first, I believed what I saw, Mama, but there's something in her eyes. I think she's being coerced…and I won't stand for a woman being used. Not after what you went through."

Aunt Maddie stood up and whispered, "Oh, Connor." She fell back into motherly tone. "You do what you must, and what your heart tells you to do." She leaned over to kiss her youngest son's forehead, then turned to Uncle

Alex and said, "We must support him in this."

Uncle Alex nodded. "We will. Whatever assistance you need in Edinburgh, you let us know. We trust you, son."

"And in England? Because I suspect that's where their trail will lead us," Connor stated.

"Wherever, Connor. Do as you must," Uncle Alex said. "Just don't be foolish. We have hundreds of guards and many allies to back you up. Use them as necessary."

Jake asked an important question, one that hadn't come to Gregor's mind. "And would King Alexander agree?"

Uncle Alex said, "Our king is in mourning. In the meantime, he trusts the Grants and the Ramsays to make sure the Highlands are safe. He'll not question our motives or our actions."

"Even if we go against the English?" Gregor asked.

"Even then. The hatred between the two kings is well-known. Everyone knows how rare it was for them to come together to support Maggie and Will's work against the Channel. Both kings will be glad for your efforts, though do not expect them to ever come together again."

"In other words, Connor, do whatever it takes," Jamie said. "Jake and I will have enough warriors for you. Send a missive with the number of guards you need, and we'll send that and fifty more." Jake nodded in agreement.

Gregor could not help but smile. The Dubh men didn't realize that the worst thing in the world had just happened to them.

Aunt Maddie had made the Channel her mission, in a way. Which meant it was also Alexander Grant's mission.

They were about to stamp out the Channel once and for all.

Connor said, "I will find out what holds those two lasses. I promise you."

They rode hard and fast and arrived on Ramsay land two

days later. That evening, Gregor pulled his half-brother, Torrian, aside and asked if he would train him out in the lists.

"Now?" Torrian asked, a reasonable question given that they were currently at a small celebration for Gregor's return from Inverness. The great hall was packed with friends and family, food and ale weighed down the trestle tables, while minstrels played a lively tune. A wedding celebration was being planned by Sorcha and Lily, who couldn't wait to share Merewen and Gavin's happiness when they arrived. Unfortunately, Gregor would miss it.

He nodded in response to his brother's question, not willing to offer an explanation yet.

Torrian tipped his head to the side as though in consideration, but then he just nodded and said, "Sure. We'll talk where there are no ears."

Grateful, he sighed and followed his brother out the door. Although Torrian likely couldn't be gone long—he was chieftain after all—the celebration would ensure their practice session stayed private.

They made their way to the stables silently, stopping to choose swords before heading toward the gates.

Once they reached the lists, Torrian asked, "Want to share what this is about? You've never been interested in swordplay, and your archery skills are nearly the best in the clan."

Considering how much he wished to share, he finally decided he didn't wish to hide anything from Torrian. He trusted him completely. "You are aware that Mama and Papa never cared whether I trained with the sword, so I chose the bow. Now, after all my travels with the cousins, I realize I'm at a disadvantage."

"Did something happen?"

He scuffed his shoe in the dirt. "I would have been killed a few nights ago, if not for Connor."

"How many?"

Gregor respected Torrian's way of getting to the heart of

the matter, one of his greatest skills as chieftain.

"Only two, but by the time I heard them, they were nearly upon me and my bow was useless."

"And the rest of the men? Our Ramsay guards were all sleeping? Because that shouldn't be and you know it."

True, Connor had thrown some sharp words at the two guards who'd neglected their duty, but in the end, it didn't matter who was at fault. He wouldn't have been any less dead. "Aye, they fell asleep. But we worked them hard the sennight before we left."

"Do not make excuses for guards. 'Tis what they train for. So your guards failed at their job, no one else heard the two reivers but you, and you blame yourself for what happened?" Torrian gave him an arch look. "'Tis admirable you wish to improve your skills, but yours is not the only mistake in this tale."

"Nevertheless, I'd like to practice my skills. I used to work in the lists, and if I could train with you a bit, I might make it to the level where I'll not embarrass myself."

"Fair enough," Torrian said, removing his tunic even in the cool night air. He'd be covered in sweat in a few moments.

There was a light breeze in the night, the tree branches waving ever so slightly. Ramsay land sat in West Lothian, on the edge of the Highlands. He loved this land, the hills and mountains, burns and glens, and everything else his clan had fought so hard to protect.

He had more to learn if he was to protect it with them.

To his surprise, Gregor found he wasn't without skill, and after several go-rounds with his brother, he believed he could hold his own in the lists. He was pleased to hear that Torrian had made the same assessment. Apparently, his increase in size over the last few years had worked to his benefit. The sword was no longer the cumbersome weapon it had been.

"Och, you're not ready for MacAdam or Connor Grant

yet, but you'll be able to defend yourself against the average reiver who swings wildly without a plan in mind."

"Many thanks, brother," Gregor said, wiping the sweat from his brow with his own tunic before he put it back on. "I feel better about it. I've not forgotten everything. You and Kyle trained me well."

"You wish to tell me why you feel the need to chase Linet?" Torrian sheathed his sword, then settled on a rock nearby, indicating he wasn't going anywhere until he had an explanation. The question didn't surprise Gregor—his mother had asked him the same thing.

He paused to gather his thoughts, then said, "This operation Linet is involved with is wrapped up with the Channel. I admire her wish to help other lasses, but I fear she's being naïve."

"You think this Sela will betray her?"

"Perhaps. It does seem she's taken a liking to Linet, but can she really rely on her for protection?"

"And your assessment of Sela? What is Connor's interest in her?"

"He seems to believe she knows more than she's telling. Linet told Merewen that Sela answers to two men, one in Edinburgh and one in London. Is it coincidence that these are the two locations Maggie has been told are cornerstones of Channel activity?"

Gregor paused, crossing his arms as he stared off into the forest, as if the answers he sought might be hiding inside.

He continued, "I think we're finally closing in on the Channel's leaders. Connor and I are both committed to leaving immediately, but we'll call in help as we need it."

Torrian nodded. "Mayhap you should talk to the Bairds before you leave. Find out why they think their daughter doesn't wish to come home. There's more to this puzzle than meets the eye. I plan to pursue the matter myself once you leave. She's a member of our clan."

"Former member of our clan."

Torrian sighed and stood up. "Not until I hear it from her lips. Why has Merewen given up so easily?"

"I don't believe she has, but the lass is exhausted. She didn't expect her sister to refuse her. Even so, after a few days' rest, I suspect she'll be eager to follow us to Edinburgh."

Torrian smirked and said, "If Gavin allows her any rest."

Gregor chuckled. "Aye, he's quite happily married. I never thought to see it this soon, but I'm happy for him. Merewen is stronger than she looks, although she's not yet capable of another long voyage. She hides her pain well, but she was dealt some nasty blows by Fitzroy in Inverness. My guess is they'll follow us within a sennight, probably about the same time Will and Maggie are ready to travel to Edinburgh."

"And you're determined not to wait for Will and Maggie?" Torrian asked. The look in his eyes told Gregor that his brother was worried for him, and he understood why. What could two warriors hope to do against one of the final outposts of the network?

He stared up at the sky, thinking of everything that had transpired in Inverness, remembering how helpless he'd felt when he, Gavin, and Connor had found Maggie and Will bound up inside a crate headed across the water. The look of them in that create—still as the dead—haunted him. For a moment, he'd feared they'd found them too late to help.

Aye, he understood why his brother was concerned, but he could not stand down, not even for a few days. He would see this through. "Seeing Maggie and Will in that crate, bound and near death, was something that'll not leave me anytime soon. I cannot let this matter rest until we find answers, and those answers lie with Sela in Edinburgh." His hands settled on his hips as he continued to stare up at the sky. "I'll practice a bit in the lists on the morrow, but we'll leave mid-day."

He pursed his lips and glanced back at Torrian. "Something tells me Linet's life could depend on it."

CHAPTER THREE

LINET HUDDLED UNDER HER MANTLE, shivering from the cold Highland wind as she and Sela led their horses down off one of the many mountains they had traversed. Three lasses trailed behind them; some of the guards were ahead of them, some behind. Linet's horse stumbled and skittered, but she patted his withers and talked him down from his panic. They were nearly through the worst of their blasted journey from Inverness to Edinburgh.

Sela, on horseback in front of her, cursed as her horse wove an unsteady path through the small stones beneath its feet. It would be a difficult fall if her horse tossed her and bolted.

"Sela, do not allow him to feel your fear. Pat him calmly," Linet called out, fearing the worst. Although usually capable of controlling her emotions, Sela wasn't an experienced rider, especially in the mountains, and the horse clearly sensed it.

Sela did her best to calm the horse, but the horse jolted down the ravine. Whether he aimed to catch the guards' horses a distance ahead of him or just get down off the mountain, they'd never know, but he bolted. Sela hung onto his mane, screeching for the beast to stop, but it only sent him into more of a lather.

They'd almost reached the bottom, where the guards at the fore of the group had stopped near a burn to water their horses, when Sela's mount decided he'd had enough of his rider. He tossed her off to the right, sending her down a small incline. One of the guards hurried over and reached for her, but she swatted at him, cursing as she pulled herself up to a standing position. "Bastard!" She glared at her horse, now standing calmly next to the others at the burn, though he did stomp his hoof once as if to remind her she'd been difficult, too.

Linet kept her horse at a controlled descent, knowing they'd be far worse off if she were thrown, too. She dismounted at the bottom and led her horse to the burn, whispering soft words to keep him calm. Once he was settled, she hurried to Sela's side. "Are you hurt?"

Sela glared at her. "Nay," she answered, brushing the stones and dry grasses from her clothing. "Foolish arse wouldn't listen to me."

"Because you are anxious and the horse senses that in you. You must try to stay calm. Take several deep breaths."

Sela did as she suggested, still glaring at her. When she finished, she threw her shoulders back. "I hate the Highlands," she stated loftily, as if the land itself had betrayed her, not her own lack of riding skill.

"You must admit 'tis quite beautiful. You'll not see a scene like this in Edinburgh."

Sela glanced at the majestic mountain they'd just descended, gray skies behind it. "True, Leena, but between the Highland savages and the steep and treacherous journey, I'd be pleased to return to the quiet of the Lowlands."

"The Lowlands?" Linet whispered. "Why?"

"Because I've lived in the Lowlands and talk like a Lowlander, and 'tis the only place I have fond memories. I could run away into the forest and live alone."

Puzzled by that admission, Linet continued her questions. Sela wasn't often willing to talk openly, much less confess anything about herself. She rarely spoke at all except to bark orders to the guards. "But I thought you were Norse…" Her physical stature—her height, her white hair and light blue eyes—all spoke to a Norse heritage.

"My sire was Scottish, my mother was Norse. Enough chatter. Calm my horse before we have to continue through this land of savages."

Linet couldn't help but be a wee bit protective of her own heritage. True, Ramsay land was very nearly in the Lowlands, but her sire had been raised a Highlander before he joined Clan Ramsay.

Sela marched over to stand in front of Linet, her hands now propped on her hips, and leaned toward her, one of her favorite intimidation tactics. "I've seen the savages, Leena, or have you forgotten? I met Connor Grant, one of the most arrogant savages I've ever met, and he's fierce with his sword, so don't try to convince me otherwise. His friends, Daniel and Gavin of who knows what clan, were brutal with their fists. They're taller than I am, their shoulders are double the width of mine, and the muscles in their arms are like boulders. They quickly dispensed with half of our guards. Nay, we need to get through this next narrow pass and closer to the Lowlands before I'll rest."

Linet wasn't swayed. "We've already passed Grant land, and they are not savages." She'd never denied Sela in such a way, and she hung her head, afraid to draw more of her leader's wrath.

"Connor Grant *is* a savage. I've been this close to him. He's powerful, ruthless, and fights like a beast. I care not to meet him in the wilderness of the Highlands. Are you certain we've passed Grant land?"

"Aye, an hour ago. Connor would not hurt you without good cause. Besides, you must admit that he and his friends are far handsomer than most men." She glanced at the guards over her shoulder, hoping they hadn't heard her.

Sela paused and Linet noticed a strange expression cross her face. Wistfulness possibly? "Aye, Connor Grant is a silent, handsome one, no denying it." She stared over Linet's head so much that Linet turned around expecting to see something, but there was nothing there.

"I'm quite certain he feels he has plenty of good cause to hurt me after what happened in Inverness. Enough talking."

Linet could swear she saw her eyes mist before she spun on her heel to talk with the guards who had been sent to escort them to Edinburgh.

"We move in five minutes."

———

After an arduous workout in the lists the next morn, Gregor moved back up toward the keep, Connor next to him, both gasping from exertion.

Connor wiped the sweat from his brow, then said, "Gregor, you've improved. Now, if I could improve that quickly with a bow, I might put more effort into it."

"Have you ever practiced with a bow?" he asked, pausing every few words for more air.

Connor chuckled. "Only a time or two at the Ramsay festivals. 'Twas quite pathetic. I gave up."

"I didn't know a Grant would give up," Gregor chided him. "Mayhap you should practice when you're with me. You could use skills at another weapon."

"I have three. Should be enough." Connor opened the door to the keep and stepped inside, holding the door for him.

"Three? Your sword and your dagger. What's your third?"

Connor smirked, "My fists. I like to wrestle with Loki or MacAdam."

Gregor headed straight for the kitchens. "Once we break our fast, I'm heading to the Bairds to talk with them about Linet. I'd like to leave for Edinburgh before the sun is highest."

"I'll be ready an hour before that. Just want to jump in the loch before we go."

Two wee voices called out to them from the trestle tables.

"Uncle Gregor, Uncle Connor!"

Lily's wee twins launched toward them at full speed, at least for their three-year-old legs. Lise jumped on Gregor and then Liliana launched herself at Connor's waist.

"Ew," Liliana said, wrinkling her nose at Connor. "I smell somepink."

Gregor's guffaws cut off abruptly as Lise quirked her lips into a strange arrangement and said, "I smell somepink, too."

Gregor said, "See that? Uncle Connor needs a bath in the loch, does he not?"

Lise shook her head vehemently.

"Nay, he does not?" Gregor asked. "But you said you smelled something."

Lise scowled then pointed at Gregor's chest. Her sister did the same.

"Me? Uncle Gregor smells?"

The twins nodded in unison.

He chortled at their blunt honesty. How he loved his wee nieces. "Guess I'll be joining you in the loch, Connor." He lifted Lise into the air with a whoop and kissed her check. "Whether you want it or not, you're getting a smelly kiss before we head to the loch." Lowering her, he did the same with her sister.

The lassies' faces lit up in unison. "May we come along, too, Uncle Gregor?" Lise whispered, as if she knew it wasn't allowed.

Her mother, Lily, strode toward them from the trestle tables. "Nay, you may not. Lads swim in the loch alone, lassies. You've finished your breakfast, now come visit with Grandmama."

Lise's face fell, but Connor reached down and mussed her hair. "'Tis way too cold for you two in the loch. Go see your grandmama."

Both lassies pushed away from their captors, their wee legs churning. Their voices echoed in the great hall, calling out, "Grandmama! Grandmama!" as they ran off toward Lily.

How much livelier things had become inside the Ramsay keep thanks to two wee lassies, and Torrian's two bairns as well, though Lily's daughters had the run of the place most of the time, making everyone smile. The thought made him wonder why Linet was not happy in Clan Ramsay. She'd always seemed to enjoy her time with Lily and the bairns, hadn't she? And he'd never met a lass who enjoyed reading more.

Did she have books wherever they'd taken her?

It struck him that the very spot where he was standing was the place where Linet had hugged him once.

Linet had grown up close by, so he'd seen her from time to time since they were wee bairns, but the first time he remembered noticing her—*really* noticing her—was the day he'd broken his arm after he and Gavin pulled a particularly foolish prank. His mother had listened to the tale of their misdeeds from Uncle Logan, who'd earned the title of the Beast of the Highlands with his raging that day, then escorted Gregor into her healing chamber. His arm had never hurt worse, but he hadn't dared say so.

They'd nearly reached the chamber when Linet came into the keep, presumably to assist with the wee ones of the clan. His mother studied her for a moment, then said, "Linet, would you mind assisting me in the healing chamber? I must straighten Gregor's arm and immobilize it for him. I could use some help."

Linet nodded at once, her eyes brightening for a moment, then took one look at him and blushed. He gathered she was excited to be assisting the mistress of her clan but embarrassed by the prospect of being close to him.

Gregor had watched many of the clan's lasses assist his mother, but none of the others possessed the patience and abilities of Linet Baird. His mother would start to ask for something, and Linet would complete the task before she'd heard the full request. She worked diligently and silently, her touch soft but skilled as if she'd been a healer for years.

Just before his mother finished the painful process of fixing his limb, Lily stuck her head inside the room and announced, "Mama, Gavin isn't allowed near Gregor for a moon. 'Tis his punishment."

"Hmmm..." his mother said once Lily left. "What shall I do with you? Your arm will make it impossible for you to help with the construction of the new huts, and you'll be no good to your brother in the lists." She thought for a moment and then glanced at Linet. Her hands settled on her hips and she asked, "Linet, haven't you been taking reading lessons with Lily?"

Linet's face lit with excitement. "Aye, we've only just started, but I love reading. I'm so hoping someday I'll be good enough to read a book on my own. I aim to teach my sister."

"You may tell your mother that I have some tasks for you at the keep for the next few weeks, and once those are done, Gregor will spend at least two hours a day teaching you how to read."

This had been Gregor's assignment or punishment, as Gavin had called it once they were allowed to speak again.

It had been far from a punishment for Gregor. Linet's hard-working spirit, her determination, and the sweet sound of her giggles whenever she struggled to make sense of a particular passage—all of it had made an impression on him. So much so that he'd crafted her a special gift as their time together had come to a close—a thin strip of wool with a whittled handle at the top.

After wrapping the package carefully and adding a book to it, he'd given it to her on the last day of their lessons.

"What is this you are giving me?" she whispered, folding her hands in front of her after she fussed with the few silky dark strands that had fallen forward. "I deserve naught. I should be giving you a gift for all your assistance and your patience."

"Nay, 'tis my appreciation for such an apt pupil. You did a fine job, and now you only need to practice to improve your new skill. Go ahead, open it."

She fumbled with the twine and the fabric covering. Her eyes misted as she carefully touched the book, her hand caressing the top cover with reverence. Then her gaze had fallen upon his creation. "'Tis most lovely, Gregor, but I'm not sure what 'tis exactly." She held it up, studying the finely rubbed wood.

"'Tis something to place between the pages of your book so you'll always know where you last ended." He reached over to demonstrate, taking the volume in his hand and showing her how to use it.

Linet Baird had set the volume down and hugged him. Her soft curves had melted against him and something had happened to him at the tender age of six and ten. He'd noticed a lass, and he hadn't yet forgotten her.

If only he hadn't been too cautious to approach her back then. To share his feelings with her. If only it weren't too late…

He rubbed his chin, appreciating this memory for what it was. Motivation to find Linet and not give up.

He had to find her.

Gregor followed the twins to greet his sister, but she shook her head adamantly. "Nay, please don't. Not until after the loch. Wee lassies don't lie, Gregor. You both smell."

He couldn't stop himself from kissing Lily's cheek—and laughing at how her nose scrunched up from the odor. "Go now…"

"We need something to eat, then we'll leave."

She waved her hand in front of her nose and said, "Come, wee lassies. We'll hide in Grandmama's favorite chamber."

The thought made him smile. His mother loved being a grandmamma. It struck him that his mother had spent a fair bit of time with Linet as well, and Linet had always seemed to admire her. She'd learned what she knew of healing from his mother.

Castle Ramsay was a happy place, was it not? What had driven Linet away?

swung his fists at him, kicking everything he could. The red-headed lad Gregor had caught fought nearly as hard as his companion, but he was a wee bit smaller.

"What brought you here?" Connor asked, holding the wriggling lad tight around the waist. "Tell me the truth and I'll let you go."

"Naught. We just wanted the loaf of bread you were eating." Even as he said it, he tried to break free.

The second lad said, "We're hungry. Please?" Scruffy as he was, he did have an honest look about him.

Gregor reached down and grabbed a loaf of bread out of the satchel still on the ground and held it out near the lad's face. "This? This is all you want?" The look of sheer want on the lad's face gave him his answer. It struck him that both boys were quite thin. He set the boy down.

"When was the last time you ate, lad?"

"Why?" Connor's boy said with plenty of attitude. "Stop asking us questions. Just give us some food and we'll leave you be. Share. 'Tis what our Lord says. We should share with others."

Connor set him on his feet and held him by the scruff of his neck. "Where do you live?"

"We live in Edinburgh," Gregor's lad said. "And we have not eaten in two days. Please, my lord?"

Now he was yanking on something inside Gregor's gut. Hellfire, but did they have to look so thin? "We'll give you the bread and the oatcakes if you stay and answer a few questions. If not, we have nearly a dozen warriors who'll chase you down."

Connor's lad said, "You won't turn us over to the sheriff?"

Connor shook his head, rubbed his chin, then said, "Nay, I'll not turn you over to the authorities. What's your name?"

"Thorn."

Connor took his hand off the lad and reached for two

seemed to admire her. She'd learned what she knew of healing from his mother.

Castle Ramsay was a happy place, was it not? What had driven Linet away?

CHAPTER FOUR

———◆———

A N HOUR LATER, GREGOR, FRESHLY washed from
the loch, headed toward the Bairds' hut. He knocked
and was quickly invited inside.

Wallace Baird stood to greet him, and Gregor nodded to
both him and his wife.

"What brings the laird's brother here?" Wallace asked, a
fine tremor in his voice. He cast an accusatory glance at
his wife.

"Just a few questions. May I?" Gregor asked, pointing to
a stool by the fire. The small flame would help him dry off
a bit quicker.

"Aye. Finnola, find the man an ale." As if accustomed to
being ordered about, she quickly hustled over to do his
bidding.

Gregor accepted the beverage with a tip of his head, then
said, "I have news of Linet, but I also have a few questions."

"I'll be heading to my smithy place in a few moments,"
Wallace said, as if to hurry him along. It mattered not—
Gregor wasn't of a mind to be rushed.

Linet's mother timidly asked, "We heard Merewen and
Gavin Ramsay are wed. 'Tis true?"

"Aye, they married in Inverness. I hope that pleases
you both. They should be here within a day or two." He
decided it best not to mention the pain Merewen was in
from her time in Inverness, the very reason they hadn't
arrived on Ramsay land yet.

"It pleases me verra much that she married our laird's nephew. He's a fine man, as are you," Wallace said, wiping the sweat on his brow with a linen square. Neither he nor his wife had settled since Gregor stepped through the door. Both continued to stand awkwardly, and Wallace would occasionally pace back and forth a few steps.

"My thanks to you," Gregor said. "You've always worked verra hard and Clan Ramsay appreciates it. I have other questions for you. Please sit," he said to them.

"Of course," Wallace said. He settled onto a stool and nodded for his wife to do the same. "I'm mighty proud of Merewen, but we've heard little else other than that Linet will not be coming with her. We were saddened she was not found."

Gregor said, "Actually, Linet *was* found. None of us spoke with her, only Merewen."

Wallace bolted back off his stool. "What? But the guards said naught. Mal and Struan asked them. Mal has been out searching on his own. He left for three days before he returned."

"We did not tell the guards. This is a personal matter, and we didn't think it appropriate for word to get around. Linet is hale and working as a healer for a woman in Inverness."

Finnola's hand went straight to her chest, and Wallace had to grab her to keep her from slipping off the stool. "She's coming home? Och, many thanks to my Lord above. Oh, I must go to chapel, tell Father Rab..."

"Nay," Gregor said, waving his hand at the woman. "She doesn't wish to come back. Merewen offered to get her out of whatever she was involved in, but Linet refused, saying she was happy there. She uses her healing skills, and she teaches the other lasses how to read."

"Books! I knew that lass would be trouble. Lasses should not be taught how to read, nor use weapons, nor..." Wallace Baird jumped out of his chair, nearly tripping over his own feet. "I've told her over and over again that she was not allowed to learn how to read. Linet and her books. Merewen and her bow."

A memory surfaced of Linet smiling down at a book, her eyes full of excitement and accomplishment. Her sire had wished to take that away from her. Anger burning in his gut, Gregor got to his feet. "I've heard enough. Your lass has one of the brightest minds I've ever known. And I'll also inform you that Merewen is an accomplished archer. She took four men out in a skirmish not far from our land. We'd have lost guards for certes had she not practiced the skills she did. I am grateful she could shoot."

"I told her she was not allowed..." Wallace's face had turned the darkest red of an autumn apple.

"Baird, I'm starting to see the problem. But before I explain, allow me to remind you that Merewen is now married. My cousin Gavin is verra happy with her skills, and I suspect they'll be practicing together often. 'Tis no longer your concern."

Fortunately, the man knew enough to close his mouth, but he let out his frustration by pacing frantically around the small hut.

"Merewen really helped? Are you sure?" her mother asked. Some emotion played in her eyes, but he could not be sure what it meant. He hoped it indicated the lasses' mother had more of an attachment to them than their sire did.

"Aye, I saw her shoot with my own eyes, and you should be proud of your daughter. I am, but that is not why I'm here. As brother to the chieftain, I'm here to ask you why you think your daughter Linet is not willing to return to Clan Ramsay. I'm concerned about her."

Finnola's gaze dropped to her hands, now folded in her lap.

"What exactly are you suggesting, Gregor Ramsay?" Wallace stood in front of him, his hands now on his large hips. He was a large man, although no longer as fit as he had been in his prime. Still, Gregor had no interest in sparring with the man.

"I'm asking you if something happened to her recently that might have caused this change in her. Was she attacked? Did she have a suitor who mishandled her? Did she have frequent nightmares? Is there something your laird should know?"

Wallace spun on his heel and walked away. "Naught. Naught has happened to make the lass feel that way. She worked hard as any of our children do, but no harder…"

His wife coughed.

"What is this?" Wallace snarled. "You deny what I say, wife?"

She fiddled with the folds in her faded wool gown, then said, "Merewen is tougher than Linet. My Linet is more tender-hearted. Physical work was hard for her, and she would put all her effort into everything. Instead of just washing the clothes in the burn, she would beat them until her knuckles were bleeding. There was no reason for her to work that hard. But I didn't think she hated it so much that…" Her hand went to her mouth and Gregor could see she was about to cry.

There was no reason for him to pursue this issue any longer. He had his answer—they knew nothing. If something had happened to Linet, she would have been far more likely to confide in Merewen than in her parents, and she had not.

He stood and said, "I just wondered. When Merewen arrives with her husband, she can tell you more about what Linet said. Of course, you understand Merewen will be living in the keep with her husband, but I'm sure they'll come to visit as soon as they are able."

Gregor nodded to both of them as Wallace moved over to wrap his arm around his wife's shoulders.

It was just as he suspected.

He'd have to unroot the truth himself.

Linet stared up at the top of the covering fashioned over the tree branches to protect her and Sela from the elements, though they hadn't had any rain at night yet. The other three lasses were in a similar structure under a nearby tree. They were getting closer to Edinburgh.

The journey had taken longer than she'd expected, probably because she'd never been on one this long before. She swiped at the dampness around her eyelids, chastising herself for being so tenderhearted.

But, oh, how she missed Winnie. Although life had always been demanding, they'd found ways to make each other happy. Linet had watched Winnie practice with her bow and arrow, marveling at her sister's ability to always hit her target exactly in the center, and Winnie had encouraged Linet's visits to Father Rab, who would allow her to read whatever he had in his library. They'd needed to keep their interests to themselves, of course. Their sire had snapped Merewen's bow in two, much like he'd ripped the pages of Linet's favorite book out and spread them across the floor. Thank goodness, the cherished gift Gregor had crafted for her had not been inside that book. She kept it well hidden to ensure its safety.

His gift had brought her through many troubling times. Whenever it felt her life was out of control, she would hold it and think of him. His patience. His finger on the parchment as he pointed to letters and phrases. His warm brown eyes, which had the power to turn her mind to mush.

Perhaps she should have let him know how she felt. There had been a time or two when she'd felt certain he was about to declare himself to her, but they'd slipped away.

She'd always hoped he would come to visit with her again, but he'd rarely been home over the past year.

She'd never told Merewen how she felt, knowing her

sister, forever a dreamer, wouldn't have let the matter rest. It was one of two secrets she'd kept from Winnie. Her feelings for Gregor? Too sweet and silly a dream to share. The other secret? Too much of a nightmare.

Now, she'd gone off with Sela, leaving her dreams and nightmares behind. She was starting to feel she'd made a mistake, although she wasn't sure what else she could have done. Go back to her home at Clan Ramsay? Never.

She squirmed in the pile of furs the men had put down for the two women, turning on her side. While the furs were better than lying directly on the hard ground, they couldn't compare to the bed she'd shared with her sister at home. Heather-filled and fragrant, she could sink into it and fall asleep in an instant.

Sleep eluded her this eve. She rolled onto her side facing Sela, accidentally brushing Sela's hand with her own in the dark.

That was a mistake.

Sela bolted up from her spot, jumped out from under the furs, screaming and swinging her arms, yelling one word over and over again.

"Spider, spider, kill the spiders. Someone, please."

The woman looked to be in a trance, still flailing her arms and bellowing about spiders as she stamped her feet. Finally, she covered her head and wailed, long and loud and full of pain.

"Sela, there are no spiders. I can't see any." She looked at the covering and didn't find anything at all.

Her assurances didn't help. The gut-wrenching screams continued, and Linet couldn't stand listening to her in such pain. She yanked on her hand. "Sela!" She shook the other woman's arm until ice-blue eyes met her gaze. "There are no spiders."

Sela's hands came up to her face as though she needed to hide from everything. Linet reached for her shoulder, but the woman shoved her away. "I'm fine. Don't touch me."

"Are you afraid of spiders? Did something happen in your past?"

"Nay. Why ask me such a ridiculous question? I can squash a spider with my hands. I thought there was a snake in my furs." She spun on her heel and headed into the forest.

The woman couldn't hide her uneven breathing from the fright she'd just had, but Linet wasn't about to press her.

One of the guards approached her and whispered, "'Tis not the first time, lass. Just ignore her. Go back to sleep. You'll need your rest by tonight. We'll be in Edinburgh by mid-afternoon."

His comment sent a bolt of fright through her.

Why would she need her rest for their first night in Edinburgh?

CHAPTER FIVE

—◆—

GREGOR AND CONNOR LEFT FOR Edinburgh shortly after arriving at Ramsay land, taking a dozen guards with them. They stopped to tend their needs midday.

"Do you think Maggie and Will have left yet?" Connor asked, chewing on mint leaves.

"Nay, they were both hurt more than they confessed. Will especially had a great deal of pain in his legs. And I doubt Maggie would push her sire to travel before he was ready."

"Aye, Uncle Logan looked verra bad, but he did make it to Inverness from Grant land."

"True," Gregor replied. "But he was driven by the powerful need to see we were all hale. Once he set eyes on Maggie and Gavin, I think he relaxed. During the battle, he willingly stayed back to protect Merewen. He needs time to recover—whether he'll admit it is another matter."

They'd stopped near a burn to water the horses. Gregor listened to the sounds of the forest—the calming sound of running water, the rustling of the leaves not as strong as usual because autumn had come and gone. Pine trees swayed with the wind, but many animals had already gone into hibernation. They'd barely seen any squirrels, although a few scurried about to gather leaves to line their dens.

It was a reminder that winter was around the corner. They'd do well to act quickly and crush the remnants of the Channel now. Otherwise, the cruel organization would have time to reorganize, something they did not want.

There was a distinct lack of any sound of horses nearby. That pleased him as he wasn't ready to test his new sword skills yet, since his shoulder muscles were still aching from his multiple practice sessions. Clouds hung low over the mountains they'd passed through, one of Gregor's favorite sights in the Highlands. He loved to look back at the mountains from the vantage point of a wide meadow. He'd asked Connor to slow at one point on their trip back to Ramsay land, just so he could take a moment to soak in the wonders of Scotland.

Connor settled onto a log, looking out at the water. "How long before Gavin convinces Merewen to follow us?"

"You mean how long before Merewen convinces Gavin to follow us?" Gregor asked with a smirk.

"True. I almost thought they would come along with us."

"Merewen is another one who hid her pain well. 'Twill be good for her to talk to her parents about Linet. When I spoke with them, neither one of them wanted to believe me." The sense that he was missing something tickled at him. He agreed with his brother—Linet had chosen not to come back for a reason. They needed to find out why, and they needed to help her.

Connor grunted. "I wouldn't want to accept that my child didn't wish to return to our clan. Not surprising on their part. I just hope we can find Linet and Sela if they're in Edinburgh. We're nearly there, though, so we should discuss where to start."

"Back in the underground. That's where we'll find them." Sela had run the underground operation in Inverness, after all—fighting rings of men and women.

Connor got up and moved to the edge of the burn, bending over to grab another clump of mint leaves. As soon as he did, an object flew past him, exactly where he would have been standing had he not bent over. He stood up and turned toward the source. "What the hell?"

Gregor stood and retrieved his bow with one hand and his sword with the other. "That was a sizable rock meant to knock you daft." He waved to the dozen guards they'd brought along to move into the periphery in the hopes they could come up behind the group of reivers. He prayed there were less than five.

Another rock landed with a large plop near the tree next to them. Gregor motioned for Connor to go closer to where it had landed, a plan in his mind.

Their satchel of food was on the opposite side of the clearing. Could that be what they were after?

He slid behind a tree not far from the food. Connor, catching on to his game, made loud comments as he turned about in a circle, trying to draw the fools' attention toward him. In a move that surprised both of them, two lads dropped out of the trees and headed straight for the food.

They threw handfuls of stones directly at Connor, who was forced to duck from the assault. Had they been men, he might have gone after them with his sword, but they were naught but laddies, and unarmed but for the stones.

Gregor caught them by surprise when he jumped out from behind the tree, grabbing one by the waist after he'd picked up a bunch of oatcakes and apples.

Connor had to chase the second one, but he caught him, herding him back to the clearing to face the inquest.

One of their guards, Owen, came over and whistled. "Lad, you made a big mistake going after these two."

They had worn their black clothing since they'd be operating as the Band of Cousins, not in their capacities as members of Clan Ramsay and Clan Grant. The guards didn't wear their plaids either.

Connor's captive—quite thin with dark, unkempt hair—

swung his fists at him, kicking everything he could. The red-headed lad Gregor had caught fought nearly as hard as his companion, but he was a wee bit smaller.

"What brought you here?" Connor asked, holding the wriggling lad tight around the waist. "Tell me the truth and I'll let you go."

"Naught. We just wanted the loaf of bread you were eating." Even as he said it, he tried to break free.

The second lad said, "We're hungry. Please?" Scruffy as he was, he did have an honest look about him.

Gregor reached down and grabbed a loaf of bread out of the satchel still on the ground and held it out near the lad's face. "This? This is all you want?" The look of sheer want on the lad's face gave him his answer. It struck him that both boys were quite thin. He set the boy down.

"When was the last time you ate, lad?"

"Why?" Connor's boy said with plenty of attitude. "Stop asking us questions. Just give us some food and we'll leave you be. Share. 'Tis what our Lord says. We should share with others."

Connor set him on his feet and held him by the scruff of his neck. "Where do you live?"

"We live in Edinburgh," Gregor's lad said. "And we have not eaten in two days. Please, my lord?"

Now he was yanking on something inside Gregor's gut. Hellfire, but did they have to look so thin? "We'll give you the bread and the oatcakes if you stay and answer a few questions. If not, we have nearly a dozen warriors who'll chase you down."

Connor's lad said, "You won't turn us over to the sheriff?"

Connor shook his head, rubbed his chin, then said, "Nay, I'll not turn you over to the authorities. What's your name?"

"Thorn."

Connor took his hand off the lad and reached for two

oatcakes. He held them out, "Thorn, aye? Son of Thor?"

The lad couldn't take his eyes off the oatcakes.

"One more question. What clan?"

Thorn locked gazes with Connor and said, "Clan Grant. Alexander Grant is my sire."

CHAPTER SIX

GREGOR EXCHANGED A GLANCE WITH his cousin, now doing his best to hide his smirk. The lad had certainly lied, but why? He decided to push the issue a bit more.

He grabbed the lad near him and asked, "And your name?"

"Nari. Son of Loki."

Gregor was so shocked he couldn't speak for a moment. Then he said, "Son of Loki. Hmmm…Loki Grant is your sire?"

Nari looked at him as if he were a fool. "Nay, son of Loki the Norse god. I'm from Clan Ramsay." He nodded emphatically as if it would convince them to believe his lie.

This could prove entertaining.

Owen came up from behind the group, a shocked expression on his face. "Did I just hear him say he's from Clan Ramsay?"

Gregor held his hand up to Owen, letting him know he was not to correct the lad. He glanced at Connor and had to look away lest he give up the jest—his cousin was covering his mouth, barely holding in his laughter.

Gregor spoke first, careful to hide his amusement by pursing his lips and crossing his arms in front of his chest. "So, one of you is from Clan Grant and the other from Clan Ramsay, yet you travel together? Why are you not with your respective clans?"

Thorn lifted his chin and said, "My sire sent me out to see what was happening in Edinburgh. I'm to report back soon. We're headed in that direction now." He crossed his arms, imitating Gregor, and even pursed his lips in the same fashion.

Nari moved closer to his friend, as if to borrow his confidence. He was clearly younger and not as quick with the lies as Thorn.

"You lie. Both of you," Connor said, crossing his arms in imitation of everyone else.

He couldn't have expected the reaction he got. "Nay, I'm not a liar!" Thorn came at him swinging his fist.

Connor caught him before he could inflict a single blow. "Whoa, lad. Don't hit me or you'll regret it. You *are* lying."

"Nay, I am from Clan Grant. *You* lie."

Gregor glanced at the lads' dirty faces, their threadbare clothing, their thin builds, and Loki Grant jumped into his mind. Before he was adopted into Clan Grant, Loki had lived on the streets in Ayrshire. His adopted son, Kenzie, had also lived on the streets. Both of them had been forced to act tougher than their years to survive. Perhaps they'd gone about this the wrong way. He ran a hand down his face, wondering how he could make things easier on the two urchins. Wouldn't he lie to feed an empty belly, especially if he were their age?

Gregor glanced at his cousin and mumbled one word to Connor, "Kenzie."

Neither boy understood him, but the word had been spoken for Connor, whose entire countenance softened. Nevertheless, he pushed along. "You're not wearing a Grant plaid, lad."

"This is an old Grant plaid, but 'tis faded."

"You're wearing a green plaid. 'Tis not a Grant plaid."

Thorn didn't lack in bravery. He took a step closer to Connor, likely the tallest man he'd ever seen, and tipped his head back to bellow at him. "How the hell would you know? You think you know so much? Wise arse comes into the burgh and thinks he's wiser than the rest of us." He then crossed his arms and stood in front of Connor, not willing to give in to him.

Connor strolled over to his horse, then led the beast over to the lads so they could see the size of his destrier, far taller than any horses in Edinburgh.

"Hell's bones, where did you find that horse?" Nari whispered, staring up at the snorting beast.

"My sire gave him to me." Connor reached into his satchel at the back of his saddle. He tugged out a length of fabric and held it up in front of the two lads. "This is a Grant plaid, lad. Not what you have on."

Thorn did all he could not to show his fear, but Nari showed enough for both of them, his eyebrows nearly touching his hairline. His gaze lingered on Connor's huge sword. "Thorn, you've crossed a Grant warrior. Please don't kill us, my lord."

"We'll not hurt you," Connor said. He held the loaf of bread out to Thorn and said, "'Tis yours but you must sit on the log and tell us where you are truly from. No more lies."

Thorn peered over his shoulder at Nari, who quickly answered, "I'll tell you all I know if I can have some bread. Please?"

The two sat on the log, and Connor and Gregor perched on a couple of rocks across from them.

Gregor waited until they'd had two bites each of the bread, just because it was so painful to see their hunger. How could one think when they were that hungry?

"So tell us who you are truly, and tell us why you are on the outskirts of Edinburgh and not inside," Connor said.

Thorn looked at his friend and muttered, "I'll tell them, Nari. Keep eating."

Gregor arched his brow at Connor. The lad was protective of his friend, an admirable quality.

"My mama died birthing me," Thorn continued. "Papa went off to sea. Said I could stay with Nari's father until he returned."

Nari butted in to finish the tale. "'Cept he's not coming back. Papa said his ship went under. He was one of the Dubh men."

Connor started to speak, but Gregor signaled for him to allow the lads to finish. He didn't wish to shut down this conversation. Any lad whose sire was in the Channel of Dubh might just have knowledge to share.

"My papa got mad because he and Thorn's papa were friends, so he went to the Dubh men and never came back."

"How long ago was that, lad?" Gregor asked.

"Two moons ago."

Thorn said, "We heard he was killed by a boar, but I don't believe them. Nari's sire could have killed a boar with his bare hands and he always had his sword." The lad stared at the ground, chewing silently. "They lied to us. Everyone lies to us."

"Where's your mama, Nari?"

"I never knew my mama. I always lived with Papa."

"How many winters are you?" Gregor asked him.

"I'm seven summers and Thorn is eight winters. He's older than me."

The lads continued to eat, not offering any more information, so Gregor decided it was time to press them. Had the lads truly stayed out here on their own for two moons? The two could have been trampled, gored, and chewed up for dinner by any number of boars. "Look, I believe your answers, but why are you not in Edinburgh? Could you not live behind an inn, or work at the stables for a place to sleep? Wouldn't it be safer?"

They both shook their head violently, their eyes wide with fear. Even Thorn had dropped the tough act. "What are you afraid of?"

Nari glanced at Thorn, who gave him a nearly imperceptible nod. "The Dubh men," Nari whispered, his voice now trembling.

"From the Channel of Dubh?" Connor asked.

"Aye. They killed our sires, and they're selling lads now. They almost got Nari, so I stole him back. Now we live out here in the forest. There's a cave we sleep in over yonder." Still protective of his friend, he didn't motion in that direction. No doubt he wished to keep it secret should they need to escape.

Nari said, "But 'tis cold and hard, and we're often hungry. Can we travel with you?"

His hopeful gaze was like a stab in his gut. The Channel had harmed so many children. Too many to count. Kenzie and Steenie had nearly been sold along with many lasses. He couldn't allow these two lads to risk their lives any longer.

He tried to meet Connor's eye, only to find his cousin was already looking at him. There was no need to ask him his thoughts. He nodded once, the movement precise.

"Well, we don't usually use them, but I'm in need of a squire," Connor said. "We may have to travel into England after Edinburgh, so I could use an extra hand with my horse and other things."

Gregor decided to go along with Connor's idea. It was the perfect way to help the lads without wounding their pride. "Nari, do you think you could act as my squire, and Thorn can be Connor's? We'll see you fed and find you a pallet at night. You have to be willing to travel, though, and you might have to split up for a short time."

"We'll do it," Thorn announced, not waiting for his friend to answer.

"Now, before you give us your answer, you would also have to help us ferret out information about this Channel of Dubh," Gregor said. "You're both small enough to enter places we cannot."

Nari's face lit up. "You mean spy on people?"

"Aye, in some situations. Spy on bad people. Do you think you could do that?"

Thorn nodded. "I can spy better than Nari, and we already know about the Channel."

"Do you know who's in charge?"

"I don't know his name," Thorn said, "but I've seen him before. And we can take you to one of their locations. They have two or three in Edinburgh."

Gregor smiled. "You lads have a deal. Lead us into the royal burgh."

Excitement transformed the lads—they looked more their age as they clapped each other's backs in excitement. "Now we really are Grant warriors," Thorn said. The two lads whooped.

Gregor shook his head. "Nay. Thorn, you're a Grant warrior, but Nari is a Ramsay warrior. Remember the difference. Someday we'll teach you the correct Ramsay and Grant war cries."

CHAPTER SEVEN

———◆———

Linet AND HER GROUP ARRIVED in Edinburgh the day after Sela fell from her horse. She had lost her tall grace to a limp, favoring her injured foot. Linet had attempted to examine her, but the woman had refused—just as she refused to speak of her night terrors.

It was already dark when the guards led them to a big stable behind a manor home not far from the middle of the burgh. There were many candles lit inside, making her wonder who awaited them within the house.

The weather had not accommodated them, instead battering them with sheets of rain most of the day. It had dropped to a constant drizzle for the last hour. Linet dismounted, shivering under her wet mantle. She and the other lasses were led through a back entrance, into a small chamber. Sela left them there without explanation. "You're not to move," was all she said. "Wait here until someone comes for you."

It sounded foreboding, especially given what the guard had told Linet. *You'll need your rest by tonight.*

The two-story manor home smelled of fresh bread, and Linet's stomach rumbled. No one spoke, although the girls exchanged a few glances. All of them looked as afraid as she felt. Finally, the door was opened by a woman with a tight black bun and eyes so brown they were nearly black. "Follow me," she said in a harsh voice. "Do not stop to speak to anyone along the way."

She did as she was told, keeping her head down as they were led into a great hall filled with people. A fire roared in the hearth and a table was weighed down with food, but the rest of the chamber held no similarities to anything she'd seen in Inverness.

Various men sat in chairs with young lasses on their laps, their hands roaming at will over their scantily clad bodies. Linet didn't know what to make of it. So shocked was she that she actually stopped moving, gaping openly at the goings on in the hall.

A hand from behind shoved at her lower back. "Have you never seen a whore before?" the lass behind her whispered. "Well, now you have. You may as well adjust yourself to it. We'll all probably be doing it soon enough. There are no fighting lasses in Edinburgh."

She turned to look at the lass, her jaw slack. The lass had a scar under her eye that did little to mar her beauty. Linet had thought to ask her about it on the road, but Sela had insisted the lasses were not to talk to one another more than was necessary. This lass's words had been harsh, but she had kind eyes.

"Whore?" was the only thing she could think to say. She had no intention of becoming a whore. "I must talk to Sela." Stories of lasses made to whore had reached her in Inverness, but she had chosen to ignore them, uncertain as to whether they were true or not. She hadn't wanted to believe Sela would force such a thing on one of them.

The girl whispered from behind her, "My name is Alys. We better get to know one another. We'll need all the friends we can get in a place like this."

"Linet. My name is Linet, but Sela calls me Leena. What did you do at Inverness? I never saw you there." She forced herself to start walking again, not wanting their harsh guide to check on them. The woman looked to be heading for the staircase at the end of the hall.

"I worked in the kitchens, but I don't know what I'll do

here. If Sela gave you that name, then you better refer to yourself as Leena. Never question her or you'll regret it."

That gave her pause. She only realized she'd stopped walking again when Alys moved ahead of her and took the lead up the staircase, tugging on her hand to make sure she followed. Her hair swung heavily against her back, and she dropped Alys's hand to reach back and squeeze out some of the water. The plaits had fallen out long ago, and the hood on her mantle had drooped off her several hours ago, leaving her drenched.

She did her best to cover a sneeze.

"Don't get sick, healer lass," Alys warned. "You'll not like it here. They'll send for someone to bleed you."

That thought sent a chill down her back. She recalled the Ramsay mistress mentioning the evil practice. Never. Never would she allow someone to bleed her. Mistress Brenna had made it well-known that she thought it a horrendous practice, one that would only make a person more ill.

They finally stepped inside a small chamber with four pallets, the last of the group to arrive. Their guide gave them a weighing look, then said, "Strip out of your wet clothes. Because of the difficult journey, you're excused from working this eve. There are clean night rails in the chest against the wall, and a vegetable pottage will be brought up soon. There is water in the two ewers, and you'll get one glass of ale with dinner to help you sleep." The woman left without offering them any additional guidance or information.

Alys led Linet to two pallets next to each other on the far wall. Although it didn't offer much in the way of privacy, a couple of thin screens separated the pallets from the table in the center of the chamber. "Get undressed and I'll find us some night rails."

She hid behind the screen and removed her clothing, folding each garment neatly. They were sopping wet, so

she left them in a small pile on the stone floor. She'd probably have to wash them on the morrow. She had one other
gown in her satchel, but it was also drenched. As soon as
she was dressed, she'd find her things and arrange them.

She was about to peek around the screen to look for
Alys when the screen was pulled back. One of the other
lasses, a favorite from the fights in Inverness, stood there
snickering. Her hair was dark and dry, though how she had
managed it, Linet would never know. Even if her hood
hadn't fallen, she'd still be drenched. This lass had ample
hips and a small bosom, though she was quite attractive.

"Well, if 'tis not the special lass, Leena. Sela won't be able
to help you here. You'll not be pampered the way you were
in Inverness, so get used to people looking at you with
naught on. No reason to be shy. Sometimes two of us take
care of one man." The look on her face told Linet she'd
hoped to shock her with her boldness.

She had. Two at once? Forcing herself to ignore the
lass, and her own vulnerable position, she focused on the
clothes on the floor.

She lifted one of her wet garments and shook it out, trying to cover her nudity, but the lass grabbed the offending
piece of clothing and flung it across the room.

Alys came around the corner of the screen to hand Linet
the night rail. Her eyes lingered on the dark-haired lass, but
she did not say aught to her. The lass didn't leave. Instead,
she crossed her arms and glared at Linet as she quickly
donned the dry garment.

"I'll leave you be. For now. But Sela won't be in charge
for long. Within a few days, you'll have a new boss. *Me*,
Ivetta." Her gaze traveled from Linet to Alys and the other
lass behind her. "You, Alys, and Maude will all do my bidding or you'll pay."

Linet wasn't willing to cross her, and apparently, neither
were the other two.

She'd made a big mistake by refusing Merewen.

Gregor hoped they'd make it to the burgh before night-fall. "Nari, know you a good inn on this side of town? I know of a few, but they are all in the middle of town." The path they were on allowed them to ride abreast of each other. Nari rode with him while Thorn sat tall in front of Connor, his eyes luminous from the excitement of riding such a large stallion. They were approaching the edge of Edinburgh.

"There's one on this side of town near the first stables. I used to take the rich guests' horses there for coin. They call it the Horse's Inn because 'tis so close to the stables."

Thorn giggled and said, "I call it the Horse's arse."

"You have a foul mouth for one so young," Connor said.

"No worse than any man," Thorn retorted.

Gregor said, "Curse all you want around us, but there will be no cursing around lasses."

"Why? Do you like lasses? Because I surely do not." Thorn's gaze narrowed as if he dared them to question his judgment.

Connor said, "For certes. You'll see someday."

The smaller lad glanced around in all directions, even behind him, before whispering, "You'll be wise to stay away from the Norsewoman."

Gregor shot a look at Connor. "And which Norse-woman is that?"

"They call her Sela and she's mean." Nari scowled as if recalling something in his past. "She has hair that's nearly white, but she's not old."

Thorn said, "He's mad because she caught him stealing apples and one of her guards walloped his butt." Turning to Nari, he added, "But she stopped him from walloping you more."

Connor listened to their exchange with interest, then said, "It surprises me to hear that. We know about Sela, too, and we've heard she's mean."

Although Connor had admitted he took a special interest in Sela's situation—that he wanted to help her if, indeed, she was being coerced into her role with the Channel of Dubh—Gregor suspected there was more to it. Lasses had always vied for Connor's attention, but he'd never shown any particular favoritism for any of them.

Sela was different. She clearly intrigued him.

"She has a soft spot for laddies, I heard," Thorn said.

"Well, I don't care," Nari whispered. "I'm not going near her."

"You need not worry about it. She's not been here for more than a moon." Thorn scratched his chin, his gaze darting around. Both of the lads were so watchful, as if danger lurked around every corner, because for them, it seemed, it did. What a sad state for a couple of laddies.

"And where exactly does the Norsewoman live?" Gregor pressed. If they found Sela, they would also find Linet—and, hopefully, the people in charge of the Channel. "Does she know the Dubh men?"

"Aye," Thorn explained. "She gives orders to the Dubh men. She sleeps in the whorehouse on the other side of town."

"Och, laddie, is there naught you don't know about? How do you know about the whorehouse?" Gregor had a sudden urge to protect the two youngsters from the harsher parts of life in a busy royal burgh.

Nari smiled. "The whores feel sorry for us and give us some of their food sometimes. But 'twas where the Dubh men found us so we have to stay away now."

The stables could be seen down at the end of the street they traveled, so Gregor asked, "Which one is the inn?"

Thorn pointed to the right side of the street. "'Tis that one. He has ten chambers abovestairs. He'll let us sleep in the small stable behind the inn. He can handle five horses."

"Good, because Midnight Moon needs to rest."

"I'll brush him for you, but it will cost you a coin," Thorn said, trying to work the two of them. His bottom lip jutted out far enough for Gregor to set the coin he'd requested on it. How he wished to chide the lad, but he held his tongue.

"No coin. You two take care of the horses while we get a room. Food is the payment you'll get. Come inside when you finish and you can eat all you want," Connor said.

Thorn's eyes widened. "All we want?"

Gregor looked at his cousin and said, "Why do I feel like you're talking with Gavin?"

Connor laughed and ruffled Thorn's dark hair. "Because this one has an appetite like Gavin. We'll see how much you can eat. In exchange for filling your belly, you'll get a bath on the morrow."

"Nay, no bath," he said with horror. "I took one last moon."

"Aye, you'll both get a bath, as will we. Lasses do not like dirty men."

"But I don't like lasses, so why must I?"

"Because you'll stink up our chamber if you don't bathe. You'd best do it while we're here. You know not where we'll be on the morrow."

"Truly?" Nari asked. "We might travel soon?" His face lit up and his gaze jumped from one to the other and back again.

He was so taken with the thought of an adventure that Gregor couldn't help but wonder if he'd ever left the city before.

"One never knows for certes," Connor said. "Take care of the horses first. My horse is Midnight Moon, Gregor's gray horse is Silver."

The lads took the horses and led them toward the back. Gregor called to them. "Do not forget you'll be leading us to the whorehouse later."

Thorn nodded. "After we eat?"

"Aye, after you eat," Connor replied. As the laddies walked away, he smirked at Gregor. "Gavin's twin."

CHAPTER EIGHT

———◆———

L INET DREAMED SHE WAS BURNING in hell. Everyone she knew stood around her, pointing at her—her
mother, her sire, her brothers, even Merewen. Winnie, as
she preferred to call her, cried out to her over and over
again. "Come back, come back, come back…please, Linet."

Behind Merewen stood Linet's abuser. "She's mine, she's
mine, she's mine…"

She just wished to run away from all of them.

A voice called to her, so she opened her eyes. Alys sat
next to her mopping her forehead. Linet almost lifted her
head off the pillow, but the other girl shook her head, the
motion just slight enough for her to see it, and pushed her
back down again. "Leena, please talk to me. I'm so afraid
for you."

Puzzled, but not wishing to upset her, Linet closed her
eyes again. She could easily sleep another few hours, but
why was Alys encouraging her to stay abed?

"Leena, wake up."

She opened her eyes, suddenly recognizing how parched
she was. "Water, please?"

"Aye, I'll get you something," Alys said, stepping over to
the chest on the side wall. "Here, drink up."

Her throat felt as if she'd swallowed a hundred thistles
in the night, so she was forced to swallow slowly. "My
throat…'tis verra sore."

"You've been quite sick." Alys took the empty goblet

and refilled it. "Have more."

Linet pushed herself to a sitting position, her gaze traveling around the empty chamber. It all came back to her—the rain, the dampness, the long journey. And here she was in Edinburgh. Ill, it would seem.

"Have you seen Sela?"

Alys shook her head. "No one has seen her since we arrived. Ivetta is being bossy, but she's not in charge yet."

"Do you think she's right? Will Sela leave us?"

"I'm not sure, but Ivetta claims the person who's in charge in Edinburgh is not so fond of her. Of course, Ivetta can't be trusted. Still, we have not seen Sela. I know we haven't had it the best, but she did do nice things for us."

"How long have I been ill?" Linet asked through the rasp in her throat. She wondered if she'd be able to talk more clearly on the morrow. Or maybe she'd lose her voice completely. Her mother had always warned her about keeping her head dry in the rain.

"You don't recall waking up this morn? I gave you something to drink, but you fell back asleep."

She handed the water goblet back to Alys.

"Do you want something to eat? I'll find you some bread or cheese. The food has been decent."

Rather than speak, she just shook her head. The thought of food made her wish to heave.

Alys urged her back down and covered her back up with the furs. "You still look like you have the fever. If you get up, you'll have to work this eve," Alys whispered. "'Tis only an hour away. Stay down for another night. They've told me that I can care for you through the night if you're still verra sick. If you're better, we'll both be sent to entertain men offering coin for us."

That was all the encouragement she needed to lie down and close her eyes again.

The next time she awakened, it was morning again.

Thorn and Nari took their new roles quite seriously and had spent the majority of the day roaming the town, listening to aught they could hear. And they'd heard quite a bit. The lads had reported seeing several Dubh men back from Inverness, along with Sela herself. There were whispers of a battle in Inverness that had gone badly wrong, so much so the local chapter of the Dubh would close down shortly and move to England.

The lads had also learned that the Dubh men had orders to take out any Ramsay, Drummond, or Grant warrior they encountered.

Once Gregor and Connor finished eating and made sure the lads had full bellies, though it had taken quite a bit to fill Thorn up to his satisfaction, they made their way into the brothel, hoping to see Linet or anyone else they might recognize.

They kept their plaids inside the satchels they carried. They needed information, so it was important to keep a low profile. Wandering through the establishment, the two grabbed a couple of ales and a bit of food while gazing at the clientele.

Gregor searched for a beautiful lass with dark hair, and there were several, but none held any interest for him. None of them were *her*. It struck him that this mission had become personal for him. Or maybe it always had been.

He couldn't get Linet out of his mind. Over the past couple of weeks, he'd had plenty of opportunities to consider what had happened between them. Their friendship had cooled after the end of their reading lessons. Once his arm had healed, he'd returned to the archery butts, practicing hard to regain the use of his arm.

The next festival they'd had, Gregor had spoken briefly with Linet, but the ease they'd developed over the course of their lessons had faded. Where once they'd talked for hours of history and the fae, that day she'd treated him as if he were little more than a stranger. Merewen had danced half the night, but Linet had sat off to the side.

Alone.

He hadn't understood it, but he'd left her, thinking that was what she wanted. Thinking she was rejecting him.

He should have been more persistent, more devoted to his cause, but he'd accepted that she wasn't interested in him. That he'd perhaps imagined the whole thing.

This time, he was determined not to let her down.

He had to try to help.

Gavin had wed his lass, but would Gregor get a chance to pursue the lass he fancied?

Foolish to even think it when she was under Sela's thrall. She might be beyond his reach forever.

"Anyone catching your eye, Connor?" he asked, when they met up back at the table filled with food.

"Nay. No Linet, no Sela."

"Do you think they've left for England already?" Gregor did his best to keep their conversation hushed, which wasn't difficult with all the giggles and drunken men surrounding them.

"'Tis possible, but I'd like to wait until Maggie and Will arrive, or even Gavin and Merewen. We need bigger numbers to shut them down."

"I feel like we're coming closer to the leaders of the Channel. If we spread word that 'tis possible, do you think all of the others would join us to put an end to these parasites?"

"I hope so," Connor said, glancing around them again. He scratched the side of his jaw, rubbing his fingers against the stubble.

Two seconds later, the ambiance in the hall changed as a hush settled over the people engaged in unsavory activities. It didn't take him long to discover what had commanded their attention.

Every face in the chamber turned toward the front door. Sela had entered.

She stood alone proudly, lifting her chin just a touch when her gaze met Connor's. Every time they were in the same room, it was as if a bolt of lightning passed from one to the other. It made him question Connor's insistence that there was naught between the two.

She wore a purple gown that was nearly black, her white hair down and flowing nearly to her waist, though she had gemstone clips near her ears to hold the strands back over her shoulders. The skirt flowed behind her and was tended by two men.

Sela had eyes only for Connor and strode directly toward him. When she reached them, she spoke one word to Connor.

"Outside." She spun on her purple slippers and never glanced back to see if he followed.

She knew he would, just as Gregor did. He couldn't consider turning her down, not when she had control of Linet. They needed her. The question was whether it would be wise to let her know they intended to help Linet.

He guessed not.

Whatever Thorn had heard about Sela's soft spot, he doubted she had one.

Connor smiled at Gregor—a small smile, more of a quirk of the lips—before he followed her.

Gregor waited until they left the hall, then made his way out through the kitchens in the back in the hopes that he could overhear their conversation without Sela noticing him.

He came around the corner just in time.

"Why did you follow me?" Sela's voice was strong and clear. He could see them from the side, her profile even more stunning.

"I didn't follow you. I traveled to Clan Ramsay, then came here with a message for our king. Don't flatter yourself."

"What message?"

"'Tis not for your ears."

She crossed her arms and was silent for a long pause. "You need to leave this establishment, Connor Grant, and never come back. Take your friends with you and stay away from me. Someday I may not be so kind."

"And what would you do to me?"

How Gregor wished he was close enough to see the expressions on their faces. They made an impressive looking couple. They were both tall, Sela nearly up to Connor's chin, which was something most men could not claim. But Connor's dark hair was the complete opposite of her light coloring. The white against the dark was such a contrast that it almost pulled them together rather than reinforced their differences.

In his eyes, good against evil.

"If I find you here again, I'll have you dragged out by my men. Aye, you have Clan Grant behind you, but they are not here to protect you, are they? Stay away or I'll have my guards give you a beating you'll not forget."

Connor's teeth were so white that his smile did show in the darkness. "Women are forced to whore for you or fight for you. How do you sleep at night? 'Tis a question I've had since I met you in Inverness. Have you no guilt for what you do?"

"None," she said, but then she leaned toward him to say something, the words spoken too quietly for Gregor to hear them.

But he did hear Connor's comment just before he strode away from her. "I look forward to teaching your men how to fight," he said, "but I'll save that fun for another night."

Sela stood at Linet's bedside the next morning and barked, "Get up." She crossed her arms over her chest and waited for a response.

When Linet was finally able to force herself to an upright position, she groaned and then waited for Sela's orders.

"Bathe and be ready within the hour. The men will take you shopping for new gowns. The ones you have are hideous and filthy. By tonight, you'll be working again." She cast her eyes downward as she went to step away.

Before she could leave, Linet burst out, "Sela, wait. As a healer? 'Tis what you have planned for me?" She chewed on her lip, awaiting her answer.

Sela stared up at the ceiling. "I am not in charge of this city as I was in Inverness. I must answer to two men, and one of them is here. You'll have to do as he tells you. No lasses fight in this city, so we have no need for a healer. You are to join the others in the hall this eve."

Linet lost all control. She grabbed Sela's hand, ignoring how the woman cringed from her touch, and begged. "Please, nay. I'll do anything you like but that. Please, Sela. I cannot be another man's whore, I cannot..."

Sela shook her hand off, though she couldn't hide the look in her eyes, an expression that made Linet think the woman was not so unfeeling as she acted. The next moment, that glimpse of emotion disappeared. "I understand," Sela said. "You were abused. Do you think you are the only woman who has ever been abused? You're not. You'll do as you're told or you'll be disciplined. I have no idea how they carry out discipline in Edinburgh. I have no control over this at all. *They* control *me*."

She left without another word.

How had Sela guessed her secret? Linet rubbed her arms, doing her best to make herself feel again, the numbness in her skin scaring her a bit. She glanced around their small chamber, but she was alone. Where were Alys, Ivetta, and Maude? All three were gone. How she wished she had someone to talk with about this decree.

Anyone.

Flouncing back onto the bed, she decided she didn't care. About anything. Any. Thing. She swiped at the tears forming on her lashes, wondering what choice she had.

She should have gone home with Merewen.

She should have told her mother.

She should have run away when she had the chance.

The door opened and a man stood in the opening. "You have five minutes to be down at the back entrance." He closed the door without waiting for a response.

And Linet did as she was told. Just like always.

CHAPTER NINE

———◆———

GREGOR AND CONNOR SAT AT the table in the main hall watching Nari and Thorn devour their porridge. Gregor said, "One more bowl, Thorn, and we must be on our way." They hoped to find some sign of Linet, or perhaps to follow Sela, if they could find her, and see where she led them.

Thorn patted his belly. "One more might fill my belly, at least, until high sun." He shoveled the rest of his bowl into his mouth and held the empty one out to be refilled.

"Do you have a hole in your toe that you're dropping all that food through?" Connor asked with a smirk.

Half an hour later, the group set out through Edinburgh, a cold gray mist shrouding the town. Gregor said, "Lads, I've a task for you. Where do the ladies in this city congregate?"

"There's a shop for the noble ladies," Nari said at once.

"Where? Take us there," Gregor said. It seemed as good a lead as any. Sela wore plenty of fine gowns.

"There's the castle, too," Thorn said. "More nobles near the castle than anywhere else."

Connor glanced at Gregor, who then said, "Thorn, you take Connor to the castle. Nari and I will go where the ladies shop."

Perhaps neither of them would find anything, but it was better to have a destination than to walk around aimlessly.

They split and walked toward their individual destinations. Gregor froze as soon as Nari led him around the final corner to the street where the shop was located.

Linet stood out like a beacon to him, the rest of the women in the area paling in comparison to her. Her beauty called to him, but the stateliness she usually emanated had fled. Even from afar, he could see she was trembling.

She wore an air of distrust and unhappiness. He had to speak to her, to ensure she was all right, although that could prove difficult. She was surrounded by about ten guards, with two other lasses inside the group.

They had no muscle, so they'd be easy to take out, but he was alone. Well, not alone but with a child nearby. What was he to do?

Nari leaned toward him to say, "You see, those lasses are headed into the manor house for gowns. They'll go in for a few hours and come out with packages."

Gregor stood to the side, hoping to catch Linet's gaze, but she was too upset to notice what was unfolding around her. She was frightened to death, if he were to guess.

He had to do something. Moving across the street from the shop, he waited to see what would happen with the guards. As he suspected, the goons stood out front, none of them following the lasses inside. He found a linen square, stepped inside a lawyer's establishment to find a writing implement, then wrote a note to Linet.

When he finished, he gave it to Nari and said, "Check for a back entrance, sneak inside, and give this to the dark-haired girl in the blue dress."

Nari gave him a serious nod, hurrying to do as he was bid. Gregor waited a few moments, then sauntered across the street to wait for Nari. If he was successful, then Linet would be coming out the back door soon.

How he prayed to see her beautiful face.

———◆———

Somehow, Linet must have gotten through to Sela. On

their way out, Sela pulled Alys aside. She didn't address Linet at all, although she gestured for her to come closer so that she might listen.

"If I have my way, your duties will change. You'll fight instead of whore. Keep that in mind and find an outfit for each of you similar to what our fighters wore in Inverness."

"Do you think 'tis possible?" Alys asked.

"I've tried to convince him before, but I was unsuccessful. You'll fight Ivetta in front of a crowd, and when he sees how the men react, he'll understand that he can make more coin from wagers than by giving you other duties."

"And Leena?"

Sela showed no emotion, but her answer was exactly what Linet had hoped to hear. "If we fight, they must have a healer. Leena is the best available to us. I'm confident he'll change his mind, but men cherish the illusion of being in control. You must also choose two regular gowns with low necklines for each of you."

A flicker of hope returned to Linet. Ivetta had changed rooms, although no one knew why. Perhaps the lass had overestimated her ability to steal Sela's position. Perhaps Sela would have her way and life would return to normal, if the lives they'd led in Inverness could be called normal. While Linet had considered trying to find her way back to Ramsay land, she'd be sick if she had to return.

She was done submitting to that kind of abuse.

Ivetta did not go to the store with them, thank goodness. Linet started to peruse the clothing with Alys and Maude when suddenly a young lad raced into the room and handed her a linen square. Befuddled, she barely had time to think before he raced out again.

Alys leaned over her shoulder as she opened the linen square, revealing the note scrawled across the inside.

Linet,
Please meet me outside. Use the back entrance. I must speak

with you.
   Gregor

Alys whispered, "What does it say?"

Since Linet doubted Alys could read, she lied. "I'm not sure. I think 'tis just from an admirer. I'm stepping outside for a moment. I need some air." She fanned her face to convince Alys of her lie.

Alys grabbed her sleeve, tugging lightly. "Leena, please be careful. If the guards see you, you'll get in terrible trouble." The look on her friend's face tugged at Linet's heart. The lass was truly concerned for her well-being.

"I promise to be careful. I still feel a wee bit sick. If I must heave, I'd rather do it out back than in here," she lied, saying a quick prayer for forgiveness.

"Would you like me to go with you?" Alys asked.

"Nay, I don't wish for you to see me in such a state." Hopefully, Alys would accept her explanation even though she'd seen the note. "If anyone asks, tell them 'tis what I'm doing."

Alys nodded, her face brightening, so Linet guessed she accepted this.

She moved through the doorway and stepped into the gray cold. Her heart pounded faster in her chest as she moved through the trees in the back, pleased to see it was presently empty. She had no idea what Gregor Ramsay wanted, but she feared it could be about Winnie or her mother, so she searched outside, surprised to see that the handsome man waiting for her was indeed Gregor Ramsay.

The boy she'd admired had become a strong, braw man, yet his eyes were still impossibly kind. Gregor gave her faith that a man could be gentle and good. She wished to touch him, but if she did, she knew she might lose the strength to stay away from him.

"Greetings to you, Gregor. Is Winnie hale?"

Gregor stepped closer to Linet so he was within arm's

reach of her—and yet, he still leaned in closer.

"What is it?" she asked.

He blushed, standing back. "Forgive me, but I caught a scent of lavender. It reminded me of when we used to read together. You smelled so sweet."

She didn't tell him that she carried a flask of lavender oil with her everywhere, putting the smallest touch on her hair whenever she washed it.

He cleared his throat and said, "Merewen is fine. She and Gavin are probably celebrating their wedding on Ramsay land."

"They married," she smiled wistfully. "I was hoping they would. Merewen deserves someone good."

"As do you. You deserve a better life than what you will be given here in Edinburgh. I've come to take you home."

Instinctively, she took a step back from Gregor. His arm reached for her, but she pulled away from him.

Gregor looked upset. "I'd never hurt you. Do you think I would?"

"Hurt me? Nay, but I was afraid you would grab me, drag me away."

Gregor scanned the area before he spoke. "'Twas foolish of me to think you would come willingly. Merewen told me you wished to stay with this group. Why? I cannot fathom why you would choose this life over a good life at Clan Ramsay."

He had no idea how much she wished to go with him, to follow him anywhere. He would protect her and take care of her, she knew that for certes, but she could not return to Ramsay land. Where else would the chieftain's own brother go? And how could Linet explain herself to Gregor? She couldn't tell him the truth—she couldn't bear it. Besides, he'd likely blame himself, or his brother.

Or…would he think it all her fault?

Too ashamed to tell the truth, she instead faltered until she could come up with a suitable explanation. "I…I…was unhappy there. While I was taken from my bed against my will, I was glad of it when I found a new life with Sela. She protects me, and I have value as a healer."

"Who took you from your bed?"

"I don't know for certes. I was given something to make me sleep. I never awoke until I was in Inverness. It does not matter."

"Aye, it does, Linet." He stepped forward and reached for her fingers, clasping them between his warm hands. "You were kidnapped, and I want to know who dared to steal you from your bed on Ramsay land. We are concerned for other lasses. I wish to find this criminal. He needs to pay for what he did to you, whether you are satisfied with your condition or not."

She couldn't fault his reasoning. She worried for others as well. But there was little she, or anyone, could do to fight this group.

"I don't know who he was. If I remember anything, I'll let you know." The heat of Gregor's body and that warm, concerned gaze began to suffuse through her. His closeness served as a warning to her. If she left with him, she'd lose her heart to him within a sennight. Nothing between them had changed—he was the brother of one chieftain and the son of another, and she was still a ruined lass unworthy of him. If she let herself love him, her heart would be broken, yet another reason why she should stay with Sela.

Gregor stepped closer, his breath now close enough to warm her face. "Linet, could there not be something between us? Did we not share something when we spent all that time together?"

She couldn't stop the nod any more than she could stop the tears that suddenly flooded her cheeks, but she quickly brushed them away. Gregor was handsome and polite, strong and virile, intelligent and protective. He would make someone a good husband, but he could never be *her* husband.

His finger touched her chin, softly lifting her gaze to his. She was lost in the chestnut brown, the color of the richest wood in the forest.

"May I kiss you, Linet? I've wanted to for a verra long time."

She lifted her chin and nodded, quelling her tears as his lips touched hers, searing her with the essence of Gregor Ramsay, probably forever. What could it hurt? She couldn't have him, but she could have this moment. It would be something to treasure, just like the gift he'd made her.

Gregor tasted of porridge, of promise, of hope, but mostly, of the good things in life. He angled his mouth and swept his tongue inside her mouth, stroking hers. Their tongues tantalized each other until she stepped back, shocked at her own lusty behavior.

She gave him a shove, and he quickly stepped back.

"Did I do something wrong?"

Linet shook her head. "Nay, Gregor. I did. Go away."

She rubbed her nose and whispered, "We can never be." And it was true. Because of what had happened to her, what had been done to her, it was unlikely any man would want to marry her. Still…how nice it had felt to step into his arms for a moment, to soak up a wee bit of his strength.

She was losing hers.

Linet made her choice and headed back into the building, her heart heavy with thoughts of brown eyes and warm lips.

The memory of Gregor Ramsay would have to last for a lifetime.

CHAPTER TEN

WHEN LINET ARRIVED BACK AT the manor home, she climbed up the stairs, still lacking the strength she had before she'd taken ill. Once in her chamber, she found the small sack of healer's salves and potions she'd brought with her to Edinburgh, going through the bag and carefully cleaning it. Hopeful that by the end of the night, she'd be a healer again, she placed it back in her sack where she could reach it quickly.

The door banged open, and Ivetta waltzed in as though she owned the chamber.

Linet jumped to her feet, afraid to see what she was about. She hadn't even spoken to the brute since the night they'd arrived.

"Did you miss me, wench? Probably not, but in case you're wondering why I didn't keep my promise, 'tis because I didn't need to." The smug look on her face told Linet she wasn't going to like whatever came next. "I just found out I'll be fighting you this eve."

Linet gave her a puzzled look but said nothing, not wishing to aggravate her.

Ivetta stepped close enough that Linet could smell her sour breath. "I'm going to kick your arse." She chucked her under the chin, then left, laughing over her shoulder.

Linet was furious. She'd had enough of being yanked around, ordered about, told what to wear, where to sleep, who to sleep with, and so many other things. Doing her best to embrace the fury rather than force it down as she usually did, she left the room and strode down the passageway, down the staircase in search of Sela. She was not in the main hall, nor in the kitchens, so she took her journey down the passageway with many doors on it, hoping to find someone she could speak with because the place seemed nearly empty.

She strode past door after door, hoping to find out where Sela was but something stopped her at one particular door near the end of the passageway. Shouting voices carried through the thick wood of the door.

Sela was arguing with a man, a familiar voice, but not one she recognized right away. She held her breath so she wouldn't miss a word of their conversation.

"Tender-hearted? What the hell do I care about tender hearts? She'll fight because I tell her to."

"You don't understand. If you wish to keep them around to fight and earn you coin, you must keep them from getting ill or injured. Leena is the best healer we've ever had. She's not capable of fighting. If you put her against Ivetta, she'll kill her and you'll have no healer."

"What the hell does she do for them but sew up the ones who need it? I can do that. She'll earn me coin like the rest of the lasses. Stop favoring her."

Linet gasped. Sela was actually standing up for her, defending her skills and her ability to heal the others.

"She has the salves that keep the fever at bay. Otherwise, you'll lose half of your fighters to poisons. You have to use her for that."

"Find out where she keeps this salve and I'll take it. You'll not change my mind, Sela. You are overstepping. Just because you handled female fighters in Inverness doesn't mean you have a head for men's business. Mind your tongue or I'll send you to England."

Sela gasped. "You wouldn't!"

"You are easily replaced. Many of the lasses would love

to have a chance to play your role. Don't push me. Do as I ask."

"But you know what would happen to me if you sent me there for the wrong reasons," Sela said, her voice breaking.

Linet couldn't help but wonder if the statuesque woman was actually close to crying.

"'Tis not my concern. I'm willing to try the fighting because I've heard the wagering is good on women, but I'll not have you trying to usurp my power here. Do as I say or face the consequences."

For so long, Linet had tried to be good. She'd stayed quiet, as she was told women should. She'd listened, even when the man speaking to her was wrong. She'd let *him* do with her as he liked, pushing down the rage, the hurt, the disquiet. She'd let the people around her convince her she wasn't good enough for the love of a man as fine as Gregor Ramsay. But something inside Linet burst when she finally recognized the bastard's voice.

Earc. He was a Ramsay guard, or at least he had been, and now he thought he could threaten Sela and tell Linet and the others what to do?

She threw the door open and slammed it closed behind her. Both faces turned toward her in shock.

"You son of a bitch," she shrieked, swearing for the first time in her life. "Earc, I recognized your voice. You're supposed to be a Ramsay guard, you traitor. You think you'll tell me what to do?" She glanced around her for a weapon and saw an array of goblets and daggers on a nearby table. Filled with rage, she grabbed whatever she could and flung it at him.

She threw one object after another, some connecting with him, some missing him because he ducked. He barked out commands that she hated. "Guards! Remove this daft woman and tie her up."

Before they came in, she charged him, slapping, biting,

and kicking everywhere she could. She must have caused him some pain because his yelling turned into bellows. She kicked him in his bollocks just before she was grabbed from behind.

"You bitch! I'll kill you for that."

Unfortunately for him, he wouldn't be killing her right away. He was too busy writhing in pain. Men attacked her from behind, grabbing both of her arms and holding her down, though she kicked and spit at will, scratching one's face and another's arm. Her fury knew no bounds.

It felt *good*.

At one point, she glanced to the side and noticed Sela standing against the wall, her expression one of shock and something else—approval? Pride?

By now, five guards had entered the room. They'd tied her up and thrown her into a chair, putting her below Earc, who'd fought his way back to his feet. His attempt at intimidation was slightly undermined by the way he covered his privates with his hands. From the look in his eyes, he was almost as angry as she was, but not quite.

He shouted, "Silence!" and the chamber quieted immediately.

First he pointed to Sela and said, "I'm sending you to England. You are banished. The man in charge of our operations can decide what to do with you. I told him 'twas foolish to allow a woman to run things." Turning to one of the guards, he said, "Take her out of here. She's allowed to get her things, but then you're to take her straight to the Borderlands. He'll decide what to do with her."

Earc waved his hand and Linet witnessed something she had not thought possible. Sela began to beg.

"Please do not send me with a bad recommendation. You know what's at stake for me, Earc. I'll go, but just reassign me. Please do not banish me."

The fear in her face made Linet almost sick to her stomach. Sela took a step toward Earc, still begging, but he slapped her ruthlessly in the face. The emotion dropped from Sela's face in an instant, her cold mask slipping back into place. She squared her shoulders. "Fine, but know that I will remember this, Earc."

She marched out the door without another glance at anyone inside, but the fear had not left her gaze. It told Linet there was much more going on in England than she cared to know. Who would a woman like Sela fear?

But this wasn't the time to worry about Sela. Once she left, Earc instructed four guards to escort her, then turned his full attention to Linet.

The first thing he did was slap her across the face. "Do not ever dare to touch me again. Aye, I was a Ramsay guard. 'Was' is the key word in this conversation. Now I am your boss, and I will run your life until my partner arrives. That starts this eve." He nodded to two guards and said, "Take her into the chamber in the cellars. At dusk, have her escorted to the fighting area in the next building. Perhaps Sela was right about one thing. These lasses will put on quite a show for us."

Earc turned to smile at her, running his finger down her jaw. "You're going to fight all night for me. Whatever happens, happens. If I'm lucky, you'll be dead by the end. In fact, I might allow wagers for the lass most likely to be dead by night's end." He snickered. "Aye, what a great idea. You'll win me tons of coins."

Linet spat at him.

How had she made such a mistake?

She knew how. Because her choices were all poor.

The guards tugged on her, forcing her to hop along behind them since her legs were tied together. When they arrived at the stairs, one of the men bent over and picked her up, tossing her over his shoulder. She kicked fast and furious, but he slapped her backside with a laugh.

The rage that had been unloosed within her still flowed freely.

"You pig," she said. "Have you no honor at all? You just beat women whenever it strikes you?"

The brute laughed and said, "Aye. 'Tis exactly what I do." All his friends laughed with him. When they reached the bottom, he tossed her onto a cot in the small room. He pointed to his peer, who grabbed a pitcher, bowl, and goblet, setting them all on the small table in the corner. A third brought in a pail and set it on the floor with a grin.

"Mayhap I'll come back and watch you use the bucket." He winked and left the cell.

The rest of the group left, shouting indecencies back at her, but she ignored them. At least Ivetta could not reach her here.

The last thing she heard was, "We'll be back to take you to your fight. Three hours, lass. Rest up."

Linet lowered her head to the pallet and sobbed.

Her world had taken a sudden turn for the worst. She'd not only lost Gregor but she'd lost her protector.

Why had she turned down Gregor's offer when she'd wanted to do anything but?

Something occurred to her. Gregor had never said why he was in Edinburgh, and if she were to guess, she'd wager he was still here. Was there any possible way she could free herself and search the burgh for him?

She had to try. Sela was headed for England to meet with a man she feared so much, the mere mention of him had reduced her to begging. That man was Earc's partner, a thought that frightened Linet more than anything.

She had to find a way out.

CHAPTER ELEVEN

GREGOR SAT IN THEIR INN, fiddling with items on the table in front of him. Their chamber abovestairs was just large enough for the four of them to sleep, so they usually convened here in the main hall to chat. It was nearly always empty.

That afternoon, he grappled with all that had transpired outside the dress shop. He'd failed Linet. He'd allowed his interest in her sway him, when he should have concentrated on convincing her to leave Sela. Clearly, she was not interested in him at all, although he could not say the same. He'd dreamed of her luscious lips all night long, dreamed of holding her close, her lavender scent enticing him.

Connor sat across from him, giving instructions to the lads. "See what you can learn at the house where the ladies are. I want to know where Linet and Sela are staying, though I doubt they're together. If you cannot find them there, then go to the house we were at before."

"The house with the whores?" Thorn asked innocently.

Gregor asked, "Why does that term not bother anyone? Nay, not the house with whores. Go to the house in the middle of town that is home to mostly women."

Nari whispered to his friend, "He means the whorehouse, does he not, Thorn?"

"Aye," Thorn replied with a whisper. "But do not call it that." They both turned back to Connor.

"If you learn anything at all, come back and tell us right

away," Connor instructed, handing them each a coin. "For a meat pie. One each."

Gregor could almost see Thorn's mouth watering. "My thanks. We'll do just as you asked."

The two disappeared, and Gregor couldn't help but smile as he stared after them. "If Loki could see those two, he'd have a laugh, would he not?"

"Aye, he would." Connor leaned back in his chair, then sat up and leaned forward. "We must talk about your experience. Why did you not bring her out anyway?"

"Because she refused. It was an odd thing. We kissed, and I could feel her passion, then she suddenly shoved at me as if I were a villain. I don't know what crossed her mind, but she told me to leave and that we could never be. How could I not do as she asked? I would never force myself on a lass."

"Nay, I'm not suggesting that. But you could have been more forceful. When someone is in the hands of those kinds of characters, they cannot think clearly. You should have brought her to a separate place, away from the women in the whorehouse. Then mayhap she would have come around."

The door opened to reveal two familiar faces. Their cousins Braden and Roddy stood outside, grinning at them. "Finally, we've found you."

Connor and Gregor jumped to their feet to greet them. "Braden, Roddy, so good to see you. We weren't expecting you," Connor said to his cousins.

"Maggie thinks we may finally be close to ending this. We said we would help when the time came."

"And how is Maggie doing? They were in rough shape in Inverness, but I think she was worse off than Will," Gregor said.

"She's better. Said to tell you they expect to arrive in another day or two. Her sire is keeping her back until he's sure she is hale. They'll bring many more guards."

Connor called for a serving lass to bring two more ales and some food. The four cousins settled in at the table, and Gregor had to admit he was pleased to see the reinforcements. It felt like they could accomplish more with greater numbers.

"In fact," Roddy said, "Maggie suspects we'll be forced to split into two locations—one group in England and one here in Edinburgh."

Braden said, "And she also said the part of the Channel in England is not in London as they first suspected but in the Borderlands. They've moved already."

"Truly?" Connor asked, surprised. "'Tis not so far from here."

"Aye," Roddy said. "We're to work with you on finding out all we can about this group in the Borderlands. Gavin and Merewen are on their way with Maggie and Will, and they'll help Gregor get Linet to safety. Maggie said she and Will would go wherever they are needed, probably here for now. What were you two discussing before we arrived? Looked to be serious."

Connor said, "'Twas most serious. Gregor spoke with Linet last eve, but she refused his help. I told him the next time he sees her, he should get her away from those people before he speaks with her. She won't agree to anything he says with her bosses watching her every move."

"He's right," Braden said. "If I'd listened to Cairstine every time she'd tried to refuse my help, we'd have never married."

Gregor groaned. "Do not forget she refused her own sister's offer of assistance in Inverness."

"True," Connor said. "But this situation is entirely different. I don't think they'll be as free to move about here. This is a large operation and Inverness was a small branch, aye, but 'tis closer to the Channel headquarters."

"I think you need to go back," Roddy said. "She's not safe with those people."

"We'll help you find her if you wish," Braden offered.

The serving lass had just set a platter of cheese and two bowls of stew in front of the men when the door flew open. The two young lads stood there, eyes wide, struggling to put their thoughts into words.

"Thorn, what have you to tell us?" Connor nudged.

Nari's eyes lingered on the newcomers, as if he weren't sure whether they could be trusted.

"You can speak freely in front of them," Gregor said. "These are our cousins, Braden and Roddy." He pointed to each of them as he made the introductions. "Braden and Roddy, meet our squires, Nari and Thorn." He shot them a look, silently promising to explain all later.

"You'll not believe it," Nari said in a quick burst. "She…" He cut himself off and stared at his friend.

Thorn finally explained what had upset them so. "Sela."

Connor stood up to move closer to the two lads. "What about her?"

"She…they… She's been *banished*. She did something they didn't like, so they're banishing her."

Thorn hopped from one foot to the other while Nari couldn't stop bobbing his head. Gregor got up and ushered the boys over to two free stools. "Calm down, lads. We'll get you some food—" he waved to the serving lass, "—then you can tell us all that transpired."

Nari took a deep breath and sat down, staring at Connor. "'Twas quite frightening to see. Sela was on horseback surrounded by a dozen guards. I've never seen that many around one prisoner."

Thorn shot Nari a scathing look. "Nari, there were only four guards. The other men on horseback were just following along to see what the group was about."

Nari stared at the floor sheepishly. "Oh, my apologies. I thought there were more."

Gregor asked, "How do you know she was a prisoner and she was not riding to some new location?"

Nari replied, "They had her hands tied but left them loose enough for her to hold the reins. And you know how Sela looks frozen all the time?"

Connor nodded. Gregor smirked at his description, though it was quite accurate.

"She looked verra upset. Upset and furious."

Gregor leaned toward Nari, placing his hand on his shoulder. "Now this is verra important. Do you know where they were headed? Did you overhear anything at all?"

"The Borderlands. 'Tis where the people following them said they were going. The guards never spoke, but other people were following them just to gawk at Sela. She cursed them all, but we ran away before she did it again," Nari said. "I don't wish to be cursed by the Ice Queen. Would she freeze me, too?"

"Nay, do not worry," Thorn patted his chest. "I'll protect you from the Ice Queen, lad." He tipped his head forward and whispered, "But they should all be wary of her. She can curse someone. She's odd. They say she's a seer or a faerie or something."

"Is that so?" Connor asked. His tone was serious, but Gregor knew him well enough to see the smirk he was fighting to contain.

Gregor recalled when they'd been young enough to be impressed with such stories.

The serving lass stepped out of the kitchen with more stew and some fruit pastries.

"Eat up, lads. You deserve it." Gregor patted Thorn's back. "Good work."

Connor took his seat again, then leaned back in his chair and glanced from Braden to Roddy. "I know you've just arrived, but we'd do best to act on this new information at once. Do you wish to travel with me?"

Gregor glanced at his cousin with a knowing smirk. "I suspected you'd be following Sela."

"Why shouldn't I? She's probably being brought to the Channel's headquarters in the Borderlands. This is what we've been waiting for all along. Don't you think so?"

"I agree. But even though she traveled with four guards, there are probably many more at the Borderlands. The three of you cannot take on twenty guards."

Connor chortled when he stood up. "Probably only ten, which is why I'll not follow directly behind them, but I wish to leave while their trail is still fresh. We don't know exactly where they are headed."

Roddy glanced at Braden and said, "We've four guards, and we'll travel with you. I think the others will be but a day behind us. You'll have reinforcements by the morrow, Gregor. Not just Will and Maggie and their guards, but Gavin and Merewen, too."

Tipping his head way back to look up at Connor from his stool, Thorn said, "What about me? You'll not leave me behind, will you? I wish to go with you. I can help spy for you."

Nari's lower lip pouted out. "I don't wanna go anywhere near the Ice Queen." He looked up at Gregor with big eyes. "I wish to help you, my lord. I'm a Ramsay guard. Can I not wait for this Maggie?"

Connor crossed his arms. "If you lads don't mind splitting up, then I'll take Thorn with me and leave Nari here to assist Gregor. He is a Ramsay, after all."

Roddy and Braden exchanged a confused look. "He is?" Roddy asked.

"We'll explain later," Gregor said. "I'd like Nari to stay. He can help me keep watch for the others."

"How would I do that? I don't know them." Nari scowled, dribbling fruit juice down his chin.

"Have you not heard of the Wild Falconer?"

Both lads stopped eating to stare at him, nodding their heads in unison. "He has those big birds, the giant ones that will attack you," Thorn said. "We heard all about him and his mean birds."

"Will is known as the Wild Falconer and he's married to Maggie Ramsay," Gregor explained. "He has two falcons who always fly overhead, but they are not that big. They only attack whomever Will tells them to go after."

"They will not go after me, will they?" Nari asked.

"Nay, not unless you attack Will."

"I will not. I promise. I'll stay here so I can meet the Wild Falconer." Satisfied that the birds weren't so great a threat as the Ice Queen, apparently, he went back to eating his fruit pie.

"Gregor, can you handle being alone for a day?" Connor asked. "Promise not to put yourself in any dangerous situations until Gavin arrives on the morrow? We have enough guards to split amongst us."

"I'll be fine. I don't think much will happen here for a couple of days." How he hoped he was right. He didn't have the skills of any of the three cousins at the table with him. If he had to use his sword, he'd be in trouble, but he wouldn't admit his worry to the others.

"Oh!" Nari bolted out of his seat and ran up to Gregor. "I almost forgot."

"What is it?"

"The lasses are fighting tonight for wagers. You must go." Nari tugged on his sleeve with a vehemence that told him the lads were getting invested in their battles. "You must."

Connor said, "Aye, you must, but that can wait until this eve. We're leaving in half an hour. Are you agreeable, Gregor?"

"Aye," he replied, though he did not relish the idea.

"Now who exactly are we chasing?" Braden asked.

"Her name is Sela," Connor explained. "The tall Norsewoman who controlled the fighting lasses in Inverness."

"Will she recognize you?" Roddy asked.

"Oh, she'll recognize me, and she will answer my questions." He pursed his lips and rubbed the palms of his hands together. "Do not doubt it."

CHAPTER TWELVE

L INET ATE THE MUSH THEY brought for her supper, deciding it was the best way to keep her strength up. Her fury at her ill treatment, and the part Earc played in it, had not ebbed one bit.

Her calm life with Sela had gone to hell, so her best bet was to try to escape, but she'd have no chance down in the cellars of the brothel. It struck her that the fighting would probably be held in this very building. The manor was large, with many chambers down here in the cellars.

In Inverness, they'd held the whoring in a separate building from the fighting, but Earc and his men hadn't had much time to arrange their new venture. It would make sense for them to use the space they already had. She had to get away somehow.

That meant she had to pretend to cooperate. If Gregor or any of his cousins were still in Edinburgh, she was certain they would return to this building.

Footsteps from the stairwell carried down to her, and the guard who had slapped her bottom appeared with a grin on his face.

She'd like to smack that grin right off his face.

"Your time is up," he said. "Here's your clothing. Put it on or I'll put it on for you." He waggled his eyebrows at her with a guffaw.

He tossed her a tight one-piece garment that fit over her body like a second skin, complete with built-in trews.

Her sire would forbid her to wear such an indecent piece of clothing, but she didn't doubt the bastard guard would love the excuse to dress her, so she turned her back and put the garment on.

"You have two minutes or I'm coming inside."

She wiggled and squirmed and finally managed to fit herself into the tight fabric, then spun around. This time, she wouldn't fight him.

Doing her best to be agreeable, she followed the brute abovestairs and then down a passageway she hadn't noticed before. She paid close attention to everything, just in case she had an opportunity to escape. This new area felt like a maze, but if she concentrated hard enough on her surroundings, she might be able to find a way out.

She passed one open area where two women were fighting, a crowd of boisterous, drunken men shouting and hollering as they hit and kicked each other. She didn't recognize either of the lasses.

They walked past more men. Most of them emerged from a large chamber down the passageway. Quite a few of them came out with goblets of ale. They all had one thing in common—they stared at her form in the tight garment. Some even whistled and tried to touch her, though the guard in front of her shoved them away.

The passageway was loud, and when they reached the end, the guard opened the door and pushed her inside, slamming it quickly behind her. Once her eyes adjusted to the dark chamber lit with only a few torches, her gaze fell on Ivetta in an outfit like hers. A sick feeling began to brew deep in her gut. The man standing next to Ivetta came to Linet's side and introduced her as "The Healer" while Ivetta had been nicknamed "Wolfette."

She'd gone over everything she'd ever heard about fighting while in her prison in the cellar—how to protect herself, how to be aggressive, and what Merewen had told her about using her legs. When the man swung his arms over his head, indicating the fight was to begin, Ivetta charged directly toward her. Linet did exactly what Merewen had said—she waited until the last minute, then stepped out of Ivetta's path and swung around to kick her in the arse.

Ivetta flew against the stone wall, but she recovered much more quickly than Linet had expected. Within seconds, she spun around with a guttural cry and said, "I'm going to kill you."

Linet thought about Earc and his partner, and her fury ignited. She waited again for Ivetta to charge toward her. This time, she bent quickly at the waist so she could get underneath her, then stood up, tossing the woman backward where she landed on the floor with an oof. The crowd went wild cheering for her. When Ivetta tried to stand, she kicked her in the belly, sending her flying backward again. This time, her head struck the stone wall and her eyes closed before she crumpled into a heap.

The man was at her side in a moment, declaring her the winner. She hoped she could leave, but a very large woman with severely plaited red hair, a beaked nose, and a frightening look of hatred entered through the doorway.

Once the fight started, she did her best to stave off the lass, who was fiercer than Ivetta, but she took several punches before she managed to strike her opponent once. She spun and connected her foot to the beast's chin. This stunned the other woman for a second, but only for a second. Then, to Linet's complete surprise, the door opened again, and Ivetta came forward to join the fight. Apparently, she'd recovered quickly from the blow to her head.

Two against one. Earc did want her dead.

She fought to the best of her ability, but it was obvious she couldn't win. She wasn't *meant* to win. And then she saw the light at the end of the tunnel.

Gregor.

He stood in the crowd of spectators—a beacon of

warmth and strength—her eyes found his in the audience. She saw the only chance she had. She shouted, "Gregor, help me, please."

And she ran straight at him.

———◆———

Gregor brought his sword with him into the fighting hall section of the brothel. Nari had chosen to wait outside the hall rather than stay in the inn alone. On the walk over, Gregor had stewed about Linet, and why she had refused him. None of the guards had been around. Had she been hesitant to leave Sela? If so, that would no longer be an issue.

If he did manage to see Linet this eve, he'd do whatever he could to speak with her. He wasn't in a position to steal her away on his own because he had no back up, but he reminded himself that she'd insisted she didn't wish to leave.

She *liked* being a healer, liked feeling she had a purpose.

He only hoped they wouldn't force her to fight. Linet was not a naturally aggressive person. It was against her nature to use fists against another person. His Linet was a quiet person who was a natural healer. Her gentle ministrations when he'd broken his arm had stayed fresh in his mind. He recalled a time when he'd escorted her home, and they had passed a baby bird that had fallen out of its nest.

He couldn't help but chuckle over that memory. He'd deemed it his duty to climb the tree to put the wee one back into its nest. The way its mother had squawked at him, he'd feared the worst, but she'd gone immediately to her baby, fussing over it like any maternal animal would do.

Linet had smiled the biggest smile he'd ever seen and said, "Do you not feel like a hero, Gregor?"

That comment had made him smile, simply because he *had* felt like a hero. Not for the bird, but for his tender-hearted Linet. Little had he recognized how powerful those moments would be for him as he grew up.

Aye, his Linet was a healer and a protector, not a fighter.

How he wished he had worked harder in the lists. True, he felt competent enough to carry his sword, but his skills were hardly on the level of his cousins'. While he could easily take on one man, maybe two, he certainly couldn't defeat every guard in the building. He'd been a fool to depend on his bow. He only hoped Linet wouldn't pay the price.

The crowd was smaller than Inverness, but the building had a larger capacity. They'd managed to fit it all in one wing of the brothel. It was arranged in a similar fashion to the fighting halls in Inverness, with a large chamber at the entrance of the wing for chatting and placing wagers. There was a small chamber toward the front of the building where two women fought, but it wasn't much of a fight. Farther down the passageway, he entered a chamber where they sold chicken legs and ale. The main fighting chamber was at the end, but nothing was going on yet. He elbowed his way back to the counter in the first chamber to make a wager.

"The Healer or Wolfette?" the man behind the counter asked brusquely. He was missing a front tooth, and the scars on his face suggested he'd lost it in a fight.

The Healer.

Gregor's heart beat faster in his chest. Were they forcing Linet to fight? Even if she had to fight tonight, he could not intervene. Not unless she needed him. He placed a bid on The Healer, grabbed an ale, and pushed his way to the back chamber just as the fighting was about to start. He wiped the sweat from his brow with his tunic sleeve as he waited for the lasses to be introduced.

Just as he'd feared, Linet was dragged into the ring, dressed in a tight one-piece outfit. He wanted to kill every last man who leered at her, but he was too worried for her to pay them much notice.

But his lassie was tough. She disabled her opponent in a few quick moves.

He expected them to lead her away, but instead another fight was announced, this time with a woman probably double her size. How would she possibly beat this brutish woman? She'd proven agile with her feet, much like Merewen, so perhaps she could stay out of the way of her opponent's fists.

The first time the other lass hit Linet, Gregor leapt out of his chair. Hellfire, but this was not going to be easy. He watched her take two more punches and a low growl came out of his chest, something he was surprised actually came from him.

Watching her made his protective instinct roar until it was ready to burst out of him. He wished to jump over all the spectators in front of him, hoist the big bitch into the air and throw her across the room. Nay, it wasn't the lass's fault—he wished to flay whoever had forced them to fight. Linet did get a couple of hits in, especially one with her foot that managed to temporarily stun the woman.

Was this what is was like to lose his heart to a lass? He ignored his inner thoughts and brought himself back to the battle in front of him. Linet's fearlessness surprised him, and so did something else—she looked furious. Her expression, usually so placid, was full of hot anger.

The door opened, and the lass from earlier emerged to join the fight. Nay! He'd not stand back and watch while two of them hurt her. He took a step forward, but before he could take another, Linet did something that shocked him. She yelled his name and headed straight for him.

"Gregor, help me!"

He held his arms open and she lunged into them, but men grabbed at her, trying to pull her back toward the fray.

"Hands away from the lady," he snapped, tucking her behind him and pulling out his sword.

"She's no lady," sneered one man.

"Never mind. You can't have her."

The spectators attacked them with taunts and jeers, but no one wanted to be on the sharp end of his sword. The guards had not caught wind of what was happening yet. He made his way toward the exit, intent on taking every advantage he had, and had almost made it when she called his name again. "Gregor!"

Three guards came at him with daggers, but Gregor had rage on his side. No one would stop him from bringing his Linet out of here safely. He finished all three of them, two with slices across their bellies and one took a deep cut to his leg. When blood started spraying, the passageway erupted into chaos. Shouting. Pushing. This was their chance. He took her hand and said, "Come. We must hurry."

Once outside the door, he yelled to his wee friend, "Nari, wait for the Wild Falconer and tell him and Maggie what has happened! We're going by horseback into the forest and headed northwest. He'll know where to find us."

Nari jumped up and down, shouting, "I will. You can count on me, my lord."

Gregor hurried Linet off to the stables to find his horse. Thanks to the tangle of people within the hall, and the ale they'd all imbibed, the guards were slow moving. He had time to retrieve his horse and toss Linet atop its back. But by the time they were galloping toward the treeline on horseback, hordes of men chased after them.

"Why are there so many?" Linet squealed. "I thought there'd only be a few of Earc's men."

"Earc? What do you mean, Earc?" Gregor must have heard her incorrectly, but he distinctly heard Earc's name. He'd suspected Earc was perhaps in the pay of the Channel of Dubh—he'd disappeared under highly suspicious circumstances in Inverness—but since when did he have his own men?

"Earc is in charge of everything in Edinburgh. He sent

Sela to the Borderlands."

Gregor nearly choked on that small piece of information. "We know about Sela. Connor and two of my cousins have gone after them, headed for the Borderlands. But this is the first I've heard of Earc."

"Earc is the one who banished her. He's the one who locked me up, who forced me to fight…"

He could feel her body shake against him, so he did his best to protect her against the cold wind. "Do not worry, Linet. I'll keep you safe whether 'tis from Earc or another."

"But are you not alone? Can we manage alone?" Her hands gripped his arms and he hoped she'd never let go.

"I'm alone for the moment. Others will be joining me soon."

She leaned back against him and clutched his arms. "Please just get me away. I don't wish to whore or fight, and I'm so, so sick of witnessing cruelty." She glanced back slightly, her face losing more color. "Where can we go? There are still so many men following us."

"Hush," he whispered, tucking her in tighter as he guided his horse. "There are plenty of caves we can hide in until my cousins arrive. Maggie and Will should be in Edinburgh on the morrow. I think Gavin and Merewen might be with them. I have a wee friend to help us out—the lad who gave you the linen square—and he'll direct them our way. Four Ramsay guards are yet at the inn. I didn't bring them to the fighting hall tonight, but they'll do their best to help us."

Linet's eyes lit up at the mention of Merewen. "I so need to see my dearest sister. She is happy with Gavin?"

"Aye, verra happy. Try to calm down so I can get us away from here. We can talk later. Can you peek over my shoulder again and tell me how many men are still following us?"

She did as he asked and she clung to his shoulders. "Four. There are four horsemen still following us."

"Then we must make this horse go a wee bit faster."

"Gregor, hurry, they're gaining on us."

CHAPTER THIRTEEN

———◆———

DESPITE THE MEN FOLLOWING FAST behind them, Linet had never felt so safe and protected before. Gregor had come for her, whisked her away from the nasty world of fighting. He cared about her and would help her return to a happier life.

If she only knew what that might look like.

Or where she might find it.

She certainly couldn't go back to her awful life on Ramsay land, so she would have to speak with Gregor about where he would take her. Of course, first they would need to lose Earc's men.

Her heart jumped into her throat as she glanced back again. "Gregor, they're almost upon us."

"Hang on, Silver will have to go faster."

"What if they catch us? What will they do?"

"I'll protect you! I have my sword, my bow, and my dagger."

"Closer...they're closer. Wait. Now they're all abreast, but one doesn't see...oh!"

"What is it?"

"One fell back. The horse's leg buckled and he tossed his rider. And the others...I cannot see them through the trees."

"Keep watch for me. 'Twill be better if I only have to fight two instead of four. Fool probably pushed his horse too far and broke its leg."

"Poor horse." She had a death grip on his bulging forearms, but it didn't seem to bother him. Afraid she'd fall off, and desperate for the reassurance of his strong body, she pressed herself as tightly to him as she could. "I think I see them again. They're still coming."

"How many?"

Linet peered over his shoulder again and said, "Three. We lost one, but two are coming faster. I fear they will catch us."

Gregor said, "I need to put an end to this because Silver may not be able to handle this pace with both of our weights. I see a perfect spot up ahead. I'm going to set you down, then I'll deal with the bastards. You can stand and hide in the trees, aye?"

"Aye."

While she had a bit of fear, she trusted him completely. If anyone could take on three men at once, it was Gregor Ramsay. When he reached the area he'd pointed to, he helped lift her down from his horse. She nearly fell, but she caught herself enough to scramble off into the bushes.

Once she was satisfied she was well hidden, she peeked out. Gregor had hidden his horse behind a group of trees. When the first two horses came barreling through the trees, Gregor swung the flat of his blade against the rider in lead, forcing him to fall off his horse in a heap. The second horse reared, and its rider fought to contain the beast.

Gregor caught him with his sword the moment the horse settled, and the bastard fell off onto his back, writhing in pain. The third horseman came along cautiously, having caught on to the ambush. To her surprise, Gregor snuck his horse around the trees and came up behind the third rider, who only had enough time to turn his horse before Gregor sliced him across his middle and he, too, fell off his horse.

When Gregor came back, he dismounted, checked to make sure the three men would not be following them, then cleaned his sword, sheathed it, and helped her back onto his horse before mounting up behind her.

She leaned against him, his arm now tight around her waist. He leaned in to whisper to her. "There's a cave not two hours from here. We can spend the night there. I don't want to go back to Edinburgh without reinforcements. Nari will get to Will and Maggie and they'll come for us on the morrow. I'm sure of it."

"Aye. Anything to get me away from them. My thanks to you, Gregor." She leaned back, her faith in this man indisputable. He hadn't given up on her—she'd sent him away, but he'd come back.

Something else was indisputable, too—she could no longer deny her feelings for Gregor. She'd enjoyed their kiss back in Edinburgh and she had a sudden desire for more. What would it be like to lie in his arms, be cradled in his warmth, his gentle touch?

Would she hate it? She feared she might, but a spark of hope lit inside her.

This desire to be closer to Gregor, to talk with him, to share her deepest feelings with him, was it because of what they'd been through or was it borne of the closeness they'd shared all those years ago? Had Merewen experienced the same thing with Gavin?

She kept glancing over his shoulder to be certain they were alone, but no horses had appeared.

After another hour, she had to hope no one else would follow them.

She was free.

She was free of the fighting, the whoring, the locked chambers, and the constant supervision. Free, also, of the demands that had been made of her at home. It felt like the first time she'd ever been truly free.

And she owed it all to the man on the horse seated behind her. Why had he risked so much for her?

Gregor eventually slowed his horse, pointing to an area

off to their right. "There's a well-hidden burn and a cave over there. Will knows it well. We'll stop here for the night." He led the horse to the burn, then dismounted before he assisted her down.

When she found her footing, she let her hands linger on Gregor's arms as she took in their surroundings. The landscape was simply gorgeous. The burn fell from a small cliff over multiple rocks, which sent its spray in many directions. The small pool at the bottom glistened in the moonlight. Surrounded by a heavy forest, she felt so protected and special.

There was nowhere else she'd rather be, no one else she'd rather be with. If she could make this moment stretch on forever, she would.

Gregor whispered, "What is it? Do you hear something?"

The only sounds were the music of the water hitting the stones and the rare song of a bird in the trees.

"Nay, Gregor, 'tis just so beautiful here. I'm in awe of it. How did you know of this place?" She stepped away from him so she could get a better look at everything—the thick trees, the meandering of the water as it left the waterfall, and the lovely stars of the night sky peeking through the tree canopy above them.

"Will and Maggie told us about a few caves not far from Edinburgh, just in case we would ever be in need. They'll know where to search for us."

He watched her as he settled his horse, his gaze following her movements.

She would be well-protected this night. "Many thanks to you for assisting me."

"I wish you had come with me when I visited you earlier, but nevertheless, I'm glad you've changed your mind. Those are not good people."

"I know. I was foolish. 'Tis hard to explain." She stared at the carpet of leaves and pine needles at her feet. Perhaps the time had come for her to tell all, but the thought of the look on Gregor's face when he learned the truth stopped her.

Not yet.

He pulled something out of his saddle bag and held it out to her. "I have an extra plaid if you'd like to don it over your garment."

She glanced at her outfit. In her haste to escape, she'd forgotten all about the tight, inappropriate garment. She brought her gaze up to Gregor, who was wearing a slight smirk, which caused her to blush the shade of the ripest apple at the top of an autumn tree. "You look fine in it, lass. Do not be embarrassed, but others may not see it that way."

"I'll take the plaid and don it after I see to my needs around the side of the cave."

He handed it to her. "I'll be right here."

Once she finished, she found Gregor rooted to the same spot. Men could just turn around and take care of everything, could they not? She watched him bend over the burn, rinse his hands and wash his face. He filled a skin with fresh water, then offered her a sip.

"I hate to hunt because I don't wish to start a fire this eve. I have a few oatcakes if that will suit you. I may have a chunk of cheese left, too. I'll leave our horse off to the side, then we can get settled in the cave."

"Do you really think they'll be along on the morrow?"

"I do."

"You trust that wee lad to find people he's never met?"

He tied his horse to a tree, ensured the animal had enough to eat, and took her hand and led the way up the small incline to the cave. Despite the other things she'd been made to do, she'd never held a man's hand like this—the warmth and heft of it made her feel cherished. The area was well-hidden in the middle of the forest, and there was no snow to show tracks. She felt safe here, with Gregor by her side.

"Aye, he's a wee sprite, quite resourceful, and we'd already explained about Will and his falcons. I told him to find the Wild Falconer and send him northwest. They'll find us."

His confidence bolstered her own.

Once they reached the opening to the cave, he held his hand up. "Allow me to go in first to make sure there are no creatures or bats inside."

She shivered and nodded, praying he wouldn't send anything large or slithery her way.

"Naught here," he said a moment later, taking her by the hand again. He led her around a corner into a large area not visible from the outside. There were several rocks arranged in such a way that they could sit on them to eat or even use one as a table. He put two furs down and pointed to them. "Go ahead and sit down." She sat on the warm furs, grateful that he was so prepared. "Here are two oatcakes for you."

They ate in silence for a moment before he said, "So I must ask you a few things, Linet. We knew each other fairly well when we were young, and the lass I knew would never have agreed to stay with Sela, as a fighter or as a healer. Do you wish to share anything? Why didn't you wish to come home?"

Linet fought the impulse to shed a few tears at the question, which was a fair one coming from the son of the previous chieftain. From her friend and one-time confidante.

She stared at the far wall of the cave. "There are things you don't know about me." Her gaze dropped to her lap.

"I would love to hear about them, not to pry into your life but because I want you to be happy. I care about you, Linet. If you'd have me, I wish to court you, but it bothers me terribly that you don't like Clan Ramsay enough to return to us. I know my brother strives to lead us well."

"'Tis not Clan Ramsay. 'Tis just…" She shivered at the memories coursing through her.

Gregor wrapped an arm around her shoulder, tucking

her in close to give her his heat. "Would it be easier if you did not have to look at me?"

She gave him a small push away from her. "Nay, I'd prefer to be able to look at you. I don't wish to be that close. 'Tis distracting."

She bit her tongue, not wishing to tell him the true reason she hated Clan Ramsay and feared the touch of a man. Before she'd been stolen from her home, she'd tried to tell Winnie about her problem. She'd always been told not to mention the visits to anyone, but she'd gotten to an age where she'd realized what was happening to her was not normal. It was not something that was done to every lass. It was wrong. And so she'd tried to tell Winnie.

She'd never gotten the chance to tell her sister. Perhaps it would be wise to tell Gregor. He was in the laird's family, after all—he could help her. If she wanted any chance at happiness in her future, she had to tell someone.

She *trusted* him.

"Will you promise not to force me to return to Clan Ramsay if I tell you?" She fiddled with the fuzz on the wool of the plaid, pondering what she was about to tell him.

"I won't force you to do anything, Linet. Ever. You have my word on that," Gregor said. "If you have been abused or mistreated in any way, you would not be the first lass who has been forced to endure such atrocities. Aunt Maddie was treated abominably by her own stepbrother before she met Uncle Alex. I could go on, but you understand what I mean. 'Tis not your fault if someone took advantage of you."

Tears burned her eyes. She didn't want her abuser to know how much he'd hurt her, how he'd stolen not just her innocence, but her self-worth. Sometimes the memories were so painful she wished to drown in misery and never speak to another soul.

The way it made her feel…

How could she explain that to anyone?

"Who, Linet? Who hurt you so badly that I can see the pain in your face? In your gaze? In every single move you make?" He moved closer and caught the first tear that meandered down her cheek with his finger, then placed a soft kiss where her cheek was still wet. "Who would treat you in such a way?"

She lifted her gaze to stare at him.

It was time to tell all, and tell all she would.

CHAPTER FOURTEEN

"WHICH OF YOU FOOLS LOST her?" The man strode into the chamber, slammed the door shut behind him, and motioned for Earc to vacate the one chair at the table. "She was one simple-minded, trembling female who was frightened of her own shadow. How could she have left this building on her own?"

Earc stood opposite the man with several of his guards, all of them silent.

"No answer? Well, you'll pay for your mistakes when I send you to the Borderlands for your punishment just the way I did Sela." He slammed a dagger down on the table for emphasis, pleased to see about half of the men jump in fear. This was exactly what he needed—fear. Nothing was a more powerful motivator. He knew that from experience—he'd used fear to control Sela, various warriors, and even Linet, although she was his favorite. Which was exactly why he was so furious she'd gotten away. "Earc reports to me on a daily basis, so keep that in mind. I have eyes that will keep me informed, and I can banish or punish any one of you fools."

"Sela will be punished for this?" one man asked, his voice carrying a slight tremor.

"Aye, she should have scared that twit silly, but instead she favored her. I could tell even from a distance. Linet is not smart enough to find a way out on her own. Someone must be at fault, and I will find out and punish them."

"She ran toward one of the spectators after two fights and left with him," Earc said. Sweat beaded on his brow. Good. "Though I didn't see the man myself, from the descriptions I was given, I suspect it was Gregor Ramsay."

"Shite. First Merewen with Gavin Ramsay and now Linet with Gregor? When the hell did they become close? Never mind. I know the answer to that question, although I thought that fancy had passed long ago. I warned her to stay away from him."

"It may have naught to do with any connection the two shared in the past. She wanted her freedom. Is that so hard to believe?" Earc said, glowering at the man behind the table.

"Aye. She's mine, and I've spent a good amount of time intimidating that lass into submission. Now I want her back. You are to do whatever you need to secure her."

"Why do you like her so much? 'Tis a sickness, I think."

The man reached across the desk and grabbed Earc by his tunic. "Say that again and you're a dead man. I'm not the only one who wants her. I just received a missive from the head of our operation in the Borderlands."

"Is he not in charge of everything in the Channel? Why should he care about one lass?"

"Aye, he is, but he needs a healer quickly. Linet is the only one we have, so I'm telling you all that you need to find her. If you don't, I'll be deciding your punishments."

———

Linet peered into Gregor's eyes as she spoke. "My brother came into my chamber one night when I was two and ten. Merewen was sleeping with Mama because she was sick. He said 'twas a brother's duty to let his sister know what would be expected of her when she grew up, to prepare her for marriage. Said he would start to teach me once I was a bit older." She peeked at Gregor to see if he doubted what she said, but she could not read anything in his gaze.

She couldn't stop her chin from quivering as the memory of that first night assailed her. Mal hadn't said anything else other than to tell her it was to be their secret. She'd never been more confused or frightened than after Mal had left her, but she'd done as she was told. Just like she always had. As her mother had oft said, she was a good lassie.

No longer.

"I don't think I need to say anything else, other than that it continued. I was miserable over it, but I didn't think there was aught I could do. I was young and didn't know any better. He insisted it was his duty and his right. I did ask lasses I met in Inverness, and they confirmed what I already suspected, that it was indeed my brother who was wrong, not me. But you know my family, Gregor. My sire thinks Mal is the best son of all, Struan is his best friend, and I would be condemned for saying anything against my own brother. But I can't live that life any longer. I wish to be free of him and never see him again." She stared at her hands in her lap, finally letting herself cry. Her tears had been held in for so very long. "I can't and I won't ever go back."

"Does Merewen know?"

"I don't believe so. I've never confided in her, though I've thought of it many times. I was trying to tell her the night I was stolen, but she had personal issues, so I decided to wait." She waited to see what Gregor would say, because she honestly had no idea.

"May I wrap my arms around you? I wish to do something, anything, to comfort you for being treated so abominably by your own family member." His gaze locked on hers. She wanted his arms around her—his touch felt warm and safe and so very different from Mal's—and yet, she struggled with wanting the touch of a male, any male.

She reminded herself that she'd seen the good in this man, time and again. He could not be more different than her brother. "Aye," she whispered, "I would like that."

He moved closer to her and wrapped one arm around her shoulder and tucked her in close under his chin, his other arm wrapping around her also. His embrace was gentle, not constricting, and she knew she could pull away if she wanted or needed to—it was part of the reason she wanted to stay right where she was.

"Linet, I want you to listen to me. You need not say a word. What your brother did to you was wrong. It is not expected behavior between a brother and sister, but between a married couple. The physical part of marriage is to be enjoyed by both the husband and the wife. 'Tis not something imposed or forced at all. True, I've heard many women do not like relations with their husband, but my sire and my brother taught me 'tis a husband's job to be certain his wife enjoys it—and that she must always be willing. Now I can't explain any more than that because I'm far from an expert, but what you speak of is wrong in every way."

She turned to stare at him because she wished to see confirmation of his words in his gaze. "Truly? You're not saying that just to make me feel better?"

"When I return to Clan Ramsay, I will banish Mal from Ramsay land."

"You would? Because of me? But he'll come after me, he'll blame me... My sire..."

"Hush," Gregor said, lifting her chin so his gaze locked on hers. "He is wrong. You are not. I'll speak with your sire, but my guess would be he has no knowledge of what transpired. I don't know any sire who would want that for their daughter. And if he feels differently, he will be banished, too. You have suffered enough."

She did the only thing she could think of to do. She wrapped her arms around Gregor and squeezed. He'd given her something she'd always treasure. He'd listened without passing judgment on her—something no amount of coin could repay.

Her conscience was clear, and she'd fallen a bit more in love with Gregor Ramsay.

———◆———

Gregor hugged her, taking in her sweet scent, and bit his lip to keep from bursting into a rage. Oh, how he'd like to kill Mal for the way he'd treated her. He'd have to be satisfied with banishing the bastard from Ramsay land—if he killed him, he suspected it would weigh heavily on Linet's conscience, something he didn't want for her.

"My thanks, Gregor, for listening." She pulled back to gaze into his eyes. "If you think I'm daft, say so, but I wish you'd kiss me."

Gregor didn't have to be asked twice, though he tamped down his desire to make sure he didn't overwhelm her. His lips touched hers hesitantly, and when she didn't pull away, he deepened the kiss, savoring her sweetness. She opened to him and he touched his tongue to hers, ever fearful she would change her mind and push him away.

Instead, a small moan came from the back of her throat and her hands reached up to the back of his neck, tugging him closer. He slanted his mouth over hers, delving deeper, and she met his pace, their tongues dueling until they were both panting. He kissed her throat, her neck, and then the small pulse just beneath her chin.

"Will you lie next to me tonight?" he asked. "I promise not to ravish you, but I'd like to hold you, know that you are hale through the night. Kissing and holding you is more than enough for me. I'm not…"

"Not what?" Her fingers ran through the thick dark strands at the base of his neck.

He took a deep breath and sighed. "I'm not as experienced as the others. My cousins have…" he paused, searching for words. How could he tell her he'd never lain with a woman? Although the opportunity had presented itself before, he'd always been too shy, and the truth was, he'd never been interested in a casual relationship.

And no lass had ever interested him as much as the one he now held in his arms.

"I don't have much experience when it comes to lasses, but I would like naught more than to hold you close while we sleep, if you'll allow it."

"I would like that. 'Struth is I'm suddenly verra tired. I thought I'd never be able to sleep, but I think I will now."

He stood and helped her to her feet, cupping her cheeks and kissing her. When he finally summoned the will to step away from her, he settled the furs in a spot against the back wall. "I'll be right back. I wish to check on our horse while I remember where I left him."

Gregor stepped outside of the cave, listening for sounds of any activity. The sun had dropped and the air had cooled considerably, but there was no indication of anything unusual going on. He rounded the side of the cave, surprised to find his horse lying flat on the ground, something he rarely did. He usually slept standing, but who was he to deny the beast a good night's sleep? Not wanting to disturb him, he returned to the cave and settled next to Linet.

"'Tis only me. All is quiet out there, so I think we can safely close our eyes." He lay down, undid his plaid though his tunic was underneath, and said, "Tuck up with your back against me, and I'll keep you warm, lass."

She smiled and leaned back against him, surprising him by putting her back flush against his chest. The soft curves of her bottom called to him briefly, but he forced those thoughts away and eased her back, her lovely scent surrounding him.

He fell asleep almost as quickly as she did.

CHAPTER FIFTEEN

WHEN LINET AWAKENED, SHE NEARLY shoved Gregor's hands away, but the memories of the previous eve flooded back to her.

She burst into a smile, savoring the feel of the man behind her, his arm wrapped tightly around her. He'd kept his word and not ravished her or done anything without telling her and asking permission.

"You slept well, lass?" His hand rubbed her arm and the sound of his voice struck a warm chord inside her. The cracks in her heart felt as if they were scabbing over.

"Aye," she murmured, not wishing to move away from Gregor's heat just yet.

"The sun is up, so I'd say we both slept well. I don't often sleep this late."

He kissed the back of her neck, his warm breath sending tingles down her neck.

"Before I do something I may regret, allow me to step outside and make sure we are safe."

She pushed forward, giving him the room he needed to stand, and handed him his plaid. He took it and wrapped it around himself deftly, then held his hand down to help her up.

She took his hand and whispered, "I need to…"

"Say no more. I do also but allow me to check the area first."

Gregor left, then returned and held his hand out to her.

"I know a spot around the side where you'll be safe. It's back near the burn so you can refresh yourself. I'm not sure what we ought to do next—wait for Will and Maggie or start our own search for them." He grinned. "Once I relieve myself, I may be able to think a bit better, and I'd also like to hear your thoughts about our plans."

Linet took Gregor's hand, and he led her to an area to the side of the cave. "I'll head in that direction. You'll have your privacy, but I'll be able to hear you. Yell if you need me." And off he went, still grinning.

Oh, how she was falling for this man. Whenever he smiled, she did.

She saw to her needs as quickly as possible, then knelt next to the burn, allowing the cold water to collect in her fingers, then splashed her cheeks and washed her face. She rinsed her mouth the best she could, then found a rock nearby, settling on it to listen to the sounds of the forest.

Even in winter the Highlands were beautiful. Bird calls still filled the air and an occasional small animal stirred the bare branches of the bushes behind her, the leaves crackling in the morning silence. The chill in the air was deep, enough that if she gave a huff, she could see her breath. Off to her left, she could see Gregor had made his way over to the part of the burn where the fresh water fell freely over a few rocks. She giggled as he tipped his face underneath the flow of water, then shook the water from his face much as a dog freed its fur of raindrops.

She'd thought him handsome before, as had nearly every other lass on Ramsay land, but her regard for him had deepened. It felt unassailable. The lad she'd admired had turned into a fine man, one who respected her and had given her hope for the future.

Where once she'd feared she'd be ridiculed and judged if anyone discovered her secret, she now felt accepted. Cherished. *Safe.*

Mal had been wrong to take advantage of her innocence.

As sure as she sat on the rock in the middle of a Highland forest, she promised herself she would never allow him to touch her again. She'd fight. From watching Sela, she'd learned how to stand up for herself, to stand tall.

Sela was a difficult woman, but she was also an inspiration.

Linet Baird no longer did as she was told.

Gregor turned and headed toward her with a smile on his face, but then he froze.

And the lovely world they'd formed together fell apart in an instant.

"Linet, get back to the cave!" he hollered. He ran to his horse, who snorted, not a good sign.

The sound of horses' hooves echoed across the land, and although she knew better—Gregor wouldn't fear *their* arrival—she still prayed it was Will and Maggie. Gregor reached for the sword sheathed on his horse, his bow already in hand. He raced toward her, his expression determined, but he was too late. An arm came out of nowhere and snaked around her waist, hoisting her into the air and onto the back of a galloping horse.

Linet fought hard. Kicking, biting, scratching, she knew she'd connected when her captor screamed, "Ow, you wee bitch!"

Earc's voice. He'd found her. He slapped her hard, but she barely even noticed—her gaze was fixed on the horses riding up behind him. Over a dozen if she were to guess. There were so many! Would they hurt Gregor? Maybe even kill him?

Gregor used his bow and took three of the men out, but the others reached him, four of them jumping down after him at the same time. He pulled his sword out and fought bravely, slicing two across the belly. They fell to the ground, but more of them jumped down to join the battle.

He fought valiantly, but he was no match for another seven men, if she counted right. Four held him and tied him up, beating him as they finished their task.

"You bastards," she screamed at Earc. "Leave us be. Have you no conscience? You're a Ramsay guard."

"I *was* a Ramsay guard. Now I'm paid well for my skills. I've no need to serve anyone." He whistled and two men left Gregor's group to attend to Earc. "Tie her up. I don't need to be kicked and scratched all the way back. She rides with me, but I want her tightly secured."

He left her with the two guards who did as he'd instructed. Earc strode over to Gregor and punched him in the face. Gregor spat blood out of the corner of his mouth. Linet kicked her legs and threw out her arms, anxious to get to him, but she couldn't break free. "I have to be tied up for you to have the courage to hit me, Earc? Why not let me go, see if you can handle me on your own? Or are you afraid of me?"

Earc's hands settled on his hips. "'Here's the truth for you. Your sister and her group have caused the Channel enough trouble. We have a huge shipment and we'll see it done. This one shipment will ensure I'll never have to work as a guard again. We're taking Linet with us. Right now, it would be too much trouble to kill you—the last thing we want is for a legion of Ramsays to come down on us—but you could quickly convince me otherwise. If you don't stop interfering, we'll do what we can to ensure your body is never found."

He moved back to his horse and mounted. "Hand her to me," he said to his friends who'd tied her. Once she was settled, too tightly bound to move much, Earc whistled for his friends to follow.

The last thing she heard was Gregor yelling, "Linet, I will follow you. This is not done, Earc. You're a dead man."

And despite the condition he was in—trussed hands and feet—she believed him.

They traveled in silence for a short time, at which point she could stand it no longer. "Why? Why can you not leave me be?"

"Because we have need of your services in the Borderlands. Quit fighting and accept your fate. Once the
shipment leaves, we won't need you any longer."

"So what then. You'll kill me?"

"Not my concern. I was instructed to get you back to
Edinburgh, then you'll be taken to the Borderlands."

Linet sighed. She knew what that meant. She would be
killed or sent out to sea. Bought and sold like a commod-
ity. But she had one small hope. If she was going to be
taken to the Borderlands, she might see Sela. If she could
manage to get under her protection until Gregor came for
her, perhaps she would survive this ordeal.

Without a doubt, she knew Gregor would come for her.
She wasn't worried about him because he was so clever
and strong. And his cousins would find him.

Just the same, she said a little prayer for him.

———————◆———————

Gregor cursed himself for his weakness. Why the hell
had he fooled himself into thinking he could protect Linet
by himself?

He'd failed her miserably.

How he prayed his cousins would be along soon, though
he hated that they'd find him in such a condition. Struggling with his ties, he did what he could, but he only
succeeding in wearing his wrists raw.

He had to do something.

*Hellfire, Ramsay! Think of something! You've always believed
your sire and mother have the quickest minds in all the clan, so
use the gift they gave you.*

He glanced over at his horse, who nickered at him, his
normal morning greeting.

"Could you not help me out, Silver?" he hollered at the
animal. "I thought you were my friend." The animal took
a step forward, giving him a light blow with his muzzle as

if cursing him for his words.

Then he noticed something. His sword lay on the ground next to his horse. The fools hadn't thought to steal his weapon. He should be able to roll over close enough to maneuver the blade between his wrists.

He rolled twice, only for Silver to take two steps closer and nuzzle him. "Shite, back up, you big beast. You're blocking my way to my sword." He had to chuckle at the animal's antics, if only to keep himself from losing his mind. "Aye, I see you feel badly for me, but no' enough to help me, aye?" He rolled again, directly at the horse's fore-leg, though he did it lightly because he knew Silver's legs were delicate. "Move, would you not?"

The horse finally took a step back with a whinny, giv-ing Gregor just enough room to do what was needed. He rolled one more time and came close enough to his blade to slip the rope binding his hands over the sharp edge, careful not to cut himself.

It took him a while, but he managed to free himself from the restraints on his wrists. That done, it was a sim-ple matter to slice the restraints on his legs. The last of the rope snapped moments before the sounds of horses' hooves reached his ears again.

His horse stepped away, lifted his nose, and then neighed—a soft, sweet sound that made Gregor sigh in relief. Silver recognized this person by smell. A friend approached him, not a foe.

Gavin rounded the cave moments later, his eyebrows arched. "What the hell happened to you, Gregor?"

His horse neighed again, this time almost in relief. When Gregor finally made it to his feet, Silver came closer and he patted the big animal's withers. "I know. 'Twas not your fault. My thanks for staying."

"What happened?" Gavin repeated. "I passed five dead men to get to you. Did you do that alone?"

"Aye." He nodded at Will and Maggie, who'd come up

behind Gavin, along with Owen and a few other guards. "But I couldn't stop the other seven from stealing Linet and tying me up."

"Linet was with you?" Maggie asked.

"Aye. After Connor, Braden, and Roddy left for the Borderlands, I went to the whorehouse to see if I could catch a glimpse of Linet. They'd set up a whole new area for the lasses to fight. When they attempted to put Linet up against two women at once, she ran straight at me and begged me to help her. So I sent Nari after you and we took off. We spent the night in the cave, hoping you'd find us this morn, but Earc and his men got here first." His throat tightened as he said those last words. Oh, he hated the memory of her on Earc's horse.

"Earc?" Owen asked. "Did you just say Earc and his men? What the hell did he want with Linet?"

Gregor explained, "Linet said Earc is one of the bosses of the Channel here in Edinburgh."

Owen growled, "I knew I didn't like that bastard."

Maggie kneaded her hands. "It must have been Earc who had Linet kidnapped. Could he be the one who arranged the attack on Will and me in Inverness?" Her gaze searched Gavin's face. "Did he send men after Papa?"

Gregor sighed and said, "Probably. One of his comments to me was that the Ramsays had caused too much trouble for the Channel. He also said the only reason he left me alive was to keep the Ramsay guards from coming down on them now. They have a huge shipment going out, and he indicated he'd earn plenty of coin from it. I'm sure he didn't expect me to be found so quickly."

"You must have surprised him. Well done if you killed five of the bastards and survived," Will said. "We'll find the lass."

Gregor nodded in acknowledgement. "Where's Merewen?" he asked Gavin.

"We left her with Nari at the inn. I promised to return

once we found you two."

A sinking sensation filled his gut. "I'm sorry I'll have to disappoint her and tell her I lost her sister."

Maggie said, "Gregor, you'll not disappoint her. You've convinced her to leave a bad situation. That will please Merewen immensely. Will's right—we'll find her."

Gregor mounted his horse, wiping some of the blood off his face with his tunic sleeve. "Aye, we will. I promised her."

The powerful need he felt to keep his promise, and soon, gave him fresh insight into why so many of his cousins had chosen to marry.

Because nothing else mattered anymore except finding Linet.

CHAPTER SIXTEEN

———◆———

B Y THE TIME THEY ARRIVED at Edinburgh, Linet thought her backside had turned raw. It wasn't easy getting off the horse with any dignity, but fortunately, Earc did not touch her inappropriately. After the wonderful night she'd spent in Gregor's arms, she didn't know if she could have handled it.

The brute untied her, then took her by the arm and shoved her inside the building she'd escaped the night before. It was clearly the whorehouse, though she'd never seen the front of it in the daylight. They moved through the front door, passed a few men having ales in the front gathering room. Everywhere she looked, there were multiple guards.

Earc took her all the way to the back of the building, down a dingy passageway with only one torch. Another passageway she'd never been down before. The manor house had plenty of surprises everywhere she looked. This part smelled of stale ale and dirty floors. Earc opened the last door to the right and stepped inside, yanking her behind him.

He then pulled her in front of him, putting her directly in the line of sight of the man seated at the table, swirling an ale and munching on stew.

Mal.

As soon as he laid eyes on her, his face lit up—completely the opposite of her reaction.

She wished to heave in the corner. Why was Mal here?

"Here you go, boss. Just like you asked. I didn't hurt her, but I did need to tie her up to get her here. She fought some, so her wrists are a wee bit raw."

Boss. Had he been working with this group of men all along?

Her brother was involved with the Channel?

Mal grinned and sauntered around the table, never taking his gaze from hers. Once he was in front, he leaned on the table and crossed his arms over his chest. "Well, well, if 'tisn't my dearest sister. Leave us," he said to Earc. "Good work. In fact, I'll leave you in charge when I have to go to the Borderlands."

The bastard grinned, nodded, and left.

Linet was so close to Mal, to her abuser, that her vision blurred. The stale aroma she'd always noticed from him invaded her nostrils, and she thought she might be sick. Blood pounded through her, so much so that she could hear the pulsation of it in her ears, a thud, thud, thud…her vision dimmed.

Her knees weakened until they nearly buckled, but the flame of hope so recently kindled inside her had not yet been snuffed out. She snapped back up straight, refusing to let his presence affect her so.

No, she would not let him have this power over her anymore.

He reached out and ran his finger down her jawline. "You're mine. I've told you that all along. I'll never allow you to be with another."

Once again, all the repressed anger and hurt welled up from where she'd hidden it, and she snapped.

Her hand came out and slapped his cheek hard, so hard that the shock in his gaze turned to a fury in a flash. But she didn't stop.

She *couldn't* stop.

Fueled by the kindness and respect of Gregor Ramsay, she swung again, hitting him three times before he grabbed her.

"What the hell's wrong with you?"

She kicked him and tried to bite his hand. "Never. You'll never hurt me again. Never! Do you hear me? Never!"

She fought for all she was worth. Mal must have decided he wouldn't be able to pacify her, because instead he grabbed her and twisted her in front of him, her back to his front. He ground out, "You're lucky you're my sister. If you were any old whore, I'd beat you silly for hitting me. But we need you in the Borderlands. You will go along with me and never do that again. Understood?"

"Nay. I'm not going anywhere with you. Send me with someone else, but not you. I hate you. You have a sickness. Leave me be. I hate you!" Her voice trembled with emotion, though she fought to contain it. She didn't want Mal to think he held that kind of control over her.

"Well, that's too bad. Merewen is in the other room tied to a chair. I suppose I'll have to take her instead of you." He pushed her down into a chair, stepping out of her way quickly. The smug look on his face told her he meant what he said.

How she wished to slap that look off his face. She jumped up to try to spit on him, but he shoved her back into the chair.

"Be verra careful. Whatever happens from here on in may be taken out on Merewen."

Frightened to her core, she sat back down and didn't move. Tears blurred her vision. "How could you? You're lying. She's not here. I don't believe you."

"Here's what I'm going to tell you, wee lass. Mayhap I am lying. But if I am, it won't be a lie for long. I'll get her away from Gavin just like I got you away from Gregor Ramsay. The Ramsay men may have been a force to be reckoned with before, but not for much longer. Now I have hundreds of men at my disposal. Why? We have the biggest shipment we've ever attempted ready to go across the waters. My bosses will spare no coin in hiring men to ensure all goes to plan. And the Ramsay guards will not pose a threat to us at all. So take a chance. Walk out that door and I'll leave you be. But know that I'll have Merewen in your place by dusk."

The tears she'd held back since Earc wrested her from Gregor finally erupted and flooded her cheeks. She bent over at the waist and covered her head with her hands because she'd heard more than she could handle. The bastards had more men than the Ramsays, and her brother wouldn't stop until he found Merewen and used her as he had Linet.

She couldn't allow it, not if there was the slightest possibility he'd be able to do as he threatened. She loved Merewen too much.

Mal knew it, too. He strode over to the door and opened it. "Make your choice, *Leena*. You either go to the Borderlands with me willingly, no hitting, or I'll leave you here and get Merewen to take your place." He held the door open for her. "What will it be?"

She lifted her head, sniffled, and said, "I'll go. Please leave Winnie alone."

"Then get up. We're leaving within the hour. Go see the woman in the next chamber and find a decent gown to wear. You cannot go in the clothes you fought in last eve. Do what you need to do and be out in front in thirty minutes. And don't forget you're now Leena again."

She lifted her gaze to give him the most loathing, hateful look she'd ever given anyone.

He reached out to chuck her under the chin. "Be kind, wee one. If you recall, we left Gregor alive. That can be changed with a flick of a dagger across his throat."

Her life no longer mattered.

———◆———

Gregor dismounted in front of their inn with a huge groan because his body ached in so many places he couldn't tell which one was the worst.

On second thought, he did know what ached the most—his heart.

He'd failed Linet and allowed her to be taken by the men from the Channel of Dubh.

Once they had all dismounted, Maggie shook her head, her gaze forlorn. "I still cannot believe Earc was a spy for the Channel. He must be the one who had Linet kidnapped."

Gavin said, "Absolutely believe it. Papa will kill him, but only after Torrian beats him until he's daft. He was right there all this time."

"He's only been with us for less than a year, Gavin," Maggie corrected him.

"True, but we've only had knowledge of the Channel for about the same amount of time."

Will motioned them inside, Nari greeting Gavin by leaping to his feet from one of the common tables. "I've protected her. She's still here, and I've allowed no one near her."

Gregor drawled, "You did a better job than I did, lad." He heaved a sigh. "I wish we had a more private place to speak, but I've not seen anyone else here other than Braden and Roddy. We'll take two more chambers now that you're here, so that could fill the inn."

Merewen stood from the table, her face so hopeful, it would break Gregor's heart to tell her the truth. He sat down next to her and said, "Merewen, Linet came to me at the fighting hall, asking for my help. We managed to escape the men from the Channel, but they caught up with us a few hours ago and stole her back."

Merewen's features tightened, but she grasped his hand and squeezed it. "But she willingly left Sela? Left her job as a healer?"

"Aye, they'd forced her to fight, and I believe 'twas too much for her. Earc was in charge of the group of men who took her. I've no notion of where she might be. Mayhap the alehouse."

Nari started waving a hand in the air to attract Gregor's attention. He looked so excited, it wouldn't surprise Gregor if he were to start jumping up and down.

The innkeeper entered the hall and said, "Ale for all? Would you like meat pies?"

"Aye, if you please," Gavin said. "The more, the better." The innkeeper nodded, but as soon as he departed, a lass brought out goblets of ale for the table.

As soon as she left, Gregor said, "What has you so excited, lad? Tell us what you've learned."

"I had to take a pish…" He glanced from Merewen to Maggie and whispered, "My apologies."

"Go ahead, Nari," Maggie said. "Tell us what you know."

"The guards said they'd look after Lady Merewen, so I hurried outside. I saw a group leaving the stables. In the middle was the lass who was with you at the alehouse, the one who had to fight. And there were two men in charge. I listened and they said they were going to the place where the others had gone."

"Who was that?" Will asked.

"Linet."

"Are you certain?" Will asked, his head tipped to the side as if he doubted the lad.

"Aye. She's the one who left with Gregor. I saw her up close!"

Quiet fell over the table as they all contemplated what that might mean. The situation had indeed come to a boil. The confrontation they'd been leading toward for months and months finally seemed upon them. Gregor just hoped Linet would not be caught in the middle of it.

Merewen was the first to speak. "I hope Sela is there. She'll protect Linet. She always has. In fact, 'twas one of the reasons Linet was willing to stay in Inverness. She trusted Sela."

"But Sela is in trouble, so where they took her is bad," Nari declared, the look on his face evidence of how much of an impression those bad men had made on him. "It may not be the same place."

The innkeeper returned with the meat pies, and they all served themselves, Gavin taking five. Although Gregor didn't feel hungry, he forced himself to eat. He'd need his strength.

"As soon as I eat, I'm going after her." He swallowed two bites in one.

"But you don't know where they're going," Gavin said. "All we know is it's in the Borderlands."

"Mayhap not, but I know where they're going," Nari said emphatically. "'Tis not a busy area. I'll be able to find Thorn, and he's with Connor, and those other two."

"Where?" Will asked, his gaze narrowing. "The Borderlands is a large area."

"South Berwick. I heard it when I was standing outside the whore…" he slapped his hand over his mouth, then dropped it quickly. "I mean the fighting hall waiting for Gregor."

Gregor and Maggie both groaned, while Gavin said, "Shite."

"What's wrong?" Nari asked. "I can take you there. We'll find them."

"South Berwick is on the River Tweed."

"Why is that bad?" he asked innocently.

Merewen's eyes misted as Maggie answered Nari's question. "Because the River Tweed leads to the sea, the most likely place for them to load their ships with lasses and lads. 'Tis a verra busy port."

Gregor swallowed the rest of his ale. "Nari, are you ready?"

"For what?" he asked, staring up at Gregor.

"We're going after them. Right away."

Nari's eyes lit up, and he nodded solemnly, leaping to his feet as Gregor did the same.

"I'm sending two guards back to Ramsay land to bring fifty back," Gregor added, looking at the others. "I'll welcome whomever wishes to come with me."

Gavin reached his hand out to help Merewen up. She'd already grabbed her bow with her free hand. "We're coming," she said, her voice throbbing with purpose.

Maggie crossed her arms. "Mayhap we should wait until the warriors arrive."

Gregor shook his head. "If we had waited, you and Will might still be in that crate on a ship in the middle of the North Sea."

Maggie's expression changed to one of fury. "You're right. Will, we leave with them. We'll send Owen and another guard back to gather the other men. They can meet us in South Berwick. We have nearly ten other guards to go with us."

"Good," Gregor said, "because I'll not wait, and I'd like your help. Connor had several guards with them because Braden and Roddy brought four. We could number a score and five. Nari, grab whatever you need. We're off."

CHAPTER SEVENTEEN

W HEN THEY ARRIVED IN SOUTH Berwick, the sun was setting. They weren't in the middle of the town as they'd been in Edinburgh and Inverness, but in an isolated area hidden inside a thick forest of trees. Linet had been forced to ride with someone she didn't know, but at least she hadn't been tied up this time. She stood outside the three buildings kneading her hands, unsure of what she'd find inside. Mal had disappeared into the front building. There were two more behind it, forming a triangle. While the one off to the left was by far the largest, the one to the right was a distance away and much smaller.

The men all spoke in low voices, but she could hear bits and pieces of what they said. The men they feared most were not here, so Mal would be in charge for the time being. It turned out her brother had not only been her tormentor, but the tormentor of many.

Mal returned from the front building and headed straight for her. Grabbing her by the elbow, he squeezed her elbow tightly and yanked her toward the largest building.

"Must you be so rough with me?" she asked through gritted teeth.

"I'll do as I wish with you. Just as I always have. You will follow all instructions without question, or you'll be assigned to my chamber." His eyes narrowed, the same way they always had whenever he'd threatened her. The cruelty inside his black heart had eaten away at his skin, leaving him a shell of the man he'd once been.

"Where is Struan?" she whispered, wondering if her other brother was a part of this travesty.

"Struan is not involved. He's too daft." He let go of her arm. "Struan almost caused a disaster. He almost caught your captors that night on Ramsay land. I had to send him off on another quest, or I would never have gotten you away."

Her heart sank. "You did all of this? My own brother arranged for my kidnapping?" She shouldn't be surprised, but even after everything he'd done, he still possessed the power to hurt her.

Ignoring her, he opened the door and shoved her into a large hall with several trestle tables in the middle. A hearth nearly filled one wall of the hall, a couple of chairs in front of it. There were only two people inside, but she recognized one because no other young person had hair that color.

Sela.

She sat in a chair in front of the hearth, her gaze staring into the flames of the fire, and didn't turn to see who had entered.

There were two other doors off the back of the hall and one at the opposite end of the hearth. The room was stark and cold. The aroma of bread baking reached her, so she guessed the closer door, the one to the right, led to the kitchens. That door opened, and a strange man came toward them, munching on a hunk of cheese. "Lock her in that chamber with Sela this eve," he said. "We'll take them in the morn."

The man gave curt instructions to another guard to bring water and food to the chamber while Mal led her inside the other door. It led to a large, and presently empty, chamber with wooden pallets that would hold at least a dozen people. He brought her around a partition that separated four beds from the others, then pointed to a pallet.

"Sit. This is where you'll stay until we need your skills on the morrow. You'll have water and food, and Sela will escort you outside to take care of your needs twice. Otherwise, don't bother me. Stay here and keep quiet."

Linet fell onto the pallet, grateful to at least be off the horse. Her backside had taken a beating in the last two days. Mal left without another word, and she said a quick prayer that he'd leave her alone until the morrow. She settled down on the rough pallet covered with a single plaid and a fur, covering up in the hopes that it would stop her trembling.

She'd dozed for a bit but was awakened by the door opening and the sound of light footsteps approaching her.

Sela came over and sat on the pallet opposite her. Linet sat up, staring at her. There was only one small torch on the wall near the door, so it was difficult to see, but she thought she saw a new sadness in Sela's gaze. There one moment, gone the next.

"Greetings, Leena," said the woman known as the Ice Queen, her demeanor once again as cold as her gaze.

Forcing herself to stay calm, she waited to see what Sela would offer. How she prayed she would give her information about why she was here.

When Sela didn't speak, Linet initiated the conversation. Waiting was torturous. "Sela. I hope you are well."

Sela's gaze was so hard Linet couldn't help but wonder what had happened in her past to make her so brusque, so unfeeling. "I prefer Inverness."

"Why am I here? I got away, but they brought me back. My own brother…"

"I had never met Mal before, but I'd heard of him. There are several men here whom you'd do best not to cross. This place…" She paused, her gaze going to the floor. "There are many more bad characters here, so tread carefully. I wish I could continue to protect you, but I cannot. They have stripped my power from me."

"Why, Sela? What is this place?"

"This is the main center of their operations. It was recently moved from London. Authorities caught on, but here…well…they can easily pay off the Lord Wardens of the Marches. They've bought silence from the English Wardens and are working on the Scottish Earls of the Marches."

"I don't understand why I'm here." She could have admitted to Sela that Mal was her brother, but she didn't want anyone to associate her with him, so she kept that information to herself.

Sela took a deep breath and heaved a sigh. "Leena, I did what I could to protect you from all of this. Have you never heard of The Channel of Dubh?"

Linet closed her eyes with a sigh, then opened them again. It was just as she'd feared. "Aye, I've heard of it, and I don't wish to be sent across the waters. Please help me. Keep me from being one of the lasses they sell."

"They don't just sell lasses," Sela said in an uncharacteristically small voice. "They sell lads as well. Anything to gain them coin. They steal whomever they can and sell them across the sea as fast as they can. This is to be a huge shipment, larger than any they've ever tried before, and they want your help."

"My help? Why? And where are they keeping all these lads and lasses?"

"You'll see on the morrow. But do not cross them. I'm warning you, unless you wish to be sold along with the others, you'll do as they say. At this point, you'll not be sent on the ship."

"But the Ramsays are here. The Grants and the Ramsays, they've brought guards. They'll try to save me, I'm certain of it."

"The men of The Channel know what they are up against. They had men implanted at Clan Ramsay so they know their numbers. They've hired enough English fighters to far outnumber the Ramsay guards. They've been preparing for this shipment for quite some time. They believe they'll earn enough money that they'll never have to work again. These cruel men will do whatever it takes to succeed. Don't cross them or they'll kill you. 'Tis that simple." She stared at a spot on the wall, her eyes glazing over. "These men…'tis a type of viciousness beyond anything I've ever seen."

Linet closed her eyes, absorbing all that she'd heard, wondering what else could possibly go wrong. Even so, she wasn't ready to give up hope. She had faith in Gregor and his family. "But you saw what happened at Inverness. The Ramsays and Grants are not to be underestimated."

"They've learned their lesson and hired more men than they think they need. What happened in Inverness did inspire them to change the location of their headquarters to South Berwick and ramp up the schedule for the shipment."

"Why do you stay?" She couldn't help but wonder why Sela would work for these kind of men.

"I have my reasons," she said flatly.

As did Linet. Her reason was Merewen.

What was Sela's?

"While you're readying the horses, I'll be right back," Nari said, dancing from one foot to another, "I have to take another…" He stopped, staring at Maggie and Merewen, trying to decide if he could use his favorite word in front of them, but then decided against it. "I'll be right back."

He dashed off toward town, knowing the perfect spot to pish in. It was his favorite because he could sometimes hit the stone on the far side of the bush with his stream. As he raced down the empty path, he pulled out his pretend sword and cut down three imaginary men who were in his way, swinging it exactly the way he'd seen Gregor do when he'd killed those bastards just inside the whorehouse. He'd snuck inside to watch. When he drove his blade into the last one's heart, he flexed his arms so they looked big like Gregor's and Connor's. Then he spat on the bastards with a snort. "Daft whoremonger bastards." He giggled a bit because he'd used two curse words, even if he was unsure what they all meant. Someday he'd be as strong as Gregor. He might even be as tall as Connor Grant. Mayhap Gregor would make him a real Ramsay guard someday.

He'd eat whenever and whatever he wanted. Even fruit pastries like they'd served them in the inn.

He found his bush and relieved himself, surprised to see a horse headed toward him. He finished his business, then glanced up at the man as he passed by.

He knew that man!

He whirled around and ran so hard down the path that his feet almost came out from under him. Gregor would be so proud of him!

He halted directly in front of Will and Maggie, who'd already mounted. One horse snorted a warning to him, but he ignored the beast, his gaze searching the area for Gavin or Gregor.

He needed to deliver his report directly to a Ramsay.

Then he glanced up at Maggie again and realized *she* was a Ramsay. For a moment he debated what to do—she was a Ramsay, aye, but she was still a lass. Lasses couldn't do what lads could. But this one was different...

"Nari?" she asked. "Something wrong?"

He heard Gregor's voice at last, so he followed it and shouted, "My lord, guess what?"

"What?" Gregor asked, tipping his head toward him.

"I found the man you all hate. I just saw him on horseback heading out of town."

"How many with him?" Gregor asked. His face had gone dark and angry, just like how Nari's sire had looked when he'd learned Thorn's sire was not coming home.

"None, he was alone."

Gregor mounted his horse and held his hand down to Nari. "Lead me to him."

"Who did he see?" Maggie asked as Gregor passed them, Nari now mounted in front of him.

"Earc. I'm going after that bastard."

Nari giggled and slapped his thigh at the curse word. He'd done a good job this time.

Mayhap he'd get a meat pie after all.

CHAPTER EIGHTEEN

———◆———

"GET UP, LINET."

Mal's voice called to her early the next morning. She rubbed her eyes and sat up in bed. The only other person sleeping behind the partition was Sela, who lay unmoving in her bed.

"You have five minutes to get yourself settled. Then meet me in the hall."

He slammed the door closed and left. At least he hadn't bothered her in the middle of the night.

She stood up and stretched, pleased to see a jug of water on the small side table. Finishing her ablutions, she wiped her teeth with a linen square and left the room, ignoring the two men sleeping on the other side of the partition.

Once she entered the hall, all talking ceased. She stepped to one side, awaiting Mal's bellow.

To her surprise, two men were seated while Mal and about a dozen others stood around them. She'd never seen either of the men before. One called out, "Agnes. Bring the lass bread and cheese."

He spoke with an English accent, as did the man beside him, who surprised her when he said kindly, "Sit, my dear."

Linet swallowed and took a seat at the table closest to her.

Apparently, that didn't suit the man in charge. "Over here, Leena," he said with a smile, tapping the table in front of him.

She did as he bid but chose a chair at the far end of the table. A woman brought her a trencher of food and a goblet of goat's milk. She thanked her and downed the milk quickly, knowing she'd probably not get much later. Gregor had reminded her that no matter what happened, she would always need to keep up her strength.

As she bit into a small wedge of cheese she'd been given, the leader of the group motioned for the other men to sit at other tables, telling the woman to feed them all porridge.

"Now, Leena. You can refer to me as Dee and this is Guy. We don't use our proper names here, just like Sela gave you a name different from the one your parents gave you. We're grateful and pleased you are finally here because we have an important job for you."

His kindness sounded false, but she'd accept it rather than the alternative. What did they want from her anyway? She would soon find out.

"We have a few lassies who have turned sick. We would like you to visit with them, tend their illness, and make them better within a few days. They're taking a journey in a sennight, and we need them to be hale and hearty by then."

Her eyes widened.

"What is it?" he asked.

"In a few days? That could be difficult depending on what kind of sickness 'tis that they carry. I have none of my potions or salves."

"We'll get you whatever you need. There are plenty of herbalists in Berwick. You will see them and tell us what will heal them. They must be ready to leave in a sennight, though we'd prefer for them to improve sooner. Do you have any questions?"

"Nay, I'll do my best." She took another bite of the bread in front of her, keeping her gaze averted, though she did her best to memorize everything about the two Englishmen.

If, no *when*, the Ramsays saved her, she'd want to give them as much information as possible.

"You have five minutes to finish. Then we go."

She nodded, not willing to question a man capable of frightening Sela and Mal. The man's shirt was dotted with dried blood, but she cared not to know where it had come from.

When she finished, she wiped her mouth with a linen square and stood. The two men immediately got to their feet. Guy said to Mal, "The three of us will go alone. Keep everyone away from us. Send more guards down the path to ensure no one comes any closer to us."

Linet kept her gaze down, refusing to look at the brother she despised as she followed the Englishmen. She'd never get away from a place with this many guards, at least not on her own.

She had to believe Gregor would find her.

The men led her to the small building off to the left, and a sound reached her ears, a horrible, heart-wrenching sound that grew louder the closer they came—bairns crying—a weak, sad cry that told her they were ill.

The first man to reach the small building opened the door. She followed him in, and the smell was so repulsive she nearly stepped back out. Both men did, holding the door open as wide as possible.

She stayed until her eyes adjusted to the sunlight casting shadows across the faces of the ill. Five bairns of varying ages under five summers lay on pallets inside. Vomit pooled in a basin at the back of the room. One woman sat in a chair staring into the distance.

"Working hard, Matilda?" Dee drawled.

"I can't help them. They heave and mess their rags. Nothing I can do for them." The look on her face told Linet exactly how hard she'd been working to help the bairns.

Linet would do all she could to help these bairns because

she knew something the others didn't. The Ramsays would attempt to save them within a sennight. She knelt down next to a child who appeared to be around three winters old. Her skin was dry and gray, her eyes vacant, her fair hair dull, but her gaze locked onto Linet as if she were the wee one's last hope.

"Mama?" the wee lass whispered.

"Nay, I'm not your mother, sweet one." She touched the child's cheeks, then placed the back of her hand against the child's forehead. That burst of heat told her the little one's body was racked with fever. She doubted the lassie would be able to lift her head off the pillow.

"Well? What must we do to heal them? Find some potion to give them to make them better." Dee's burst of instructions sounded as cold as she would have expected.

This was not as simple as giving them a potion. Her guess was that because they'd been underfed, they'd caught something, and it had spread amongst them.

Linet stood back up and stepped outside the building, the door still propped open. "What have you been feeding them?"

Guy looked to Matilda. "Answer her question."

"Naught. I've given them naught because they just heave it or send it out their back end."

He glanced back to Linet and raised his brows.

"I know not what they have," she said, "but they are thirsty and starving to death. If you don't give them some liquid, goat's milk or something, they'll die. Once a child stops heaving, you must give them something to drink. 'Tis the most important potion according to my mistress."

"I think we should bleed them. 'Tis the most common practice," Dee added.

"Nay!" Linet insisted. Mayhap she'd be punished for her boldness, but they'd asked her to cure the bairns. "If you do so, they'll be dying by the morrow. None are heaving now so you must feed them. How about broth? Allow them to drink mutton broth or something similar." She recalled how upset Mistress Brenna had become at the mention of bleeding a bairn at the Ramsay keep. That refusal had always stayed in her mind.

"How do we do that? They're barely awake," Matilda said.

"If someone brings us broth, I shall assist you in feeding them."

The two men exchanged a look, and Guy nodded to Dee and left. Dee, the one who'd acted so kindly, said, "He'll see it done. I'll be back to check on the bairns on the morrow, and if they're not better, I'll consider it your fault." He spun on his heel and left, closing the door behind him.

Linet stood outside the small building, leaning back against the cold stone for support. Her knees had weakened and her belly churned, all due to a thought she'd had.

A thought that she believed with a certainty that frightened her.

If there were five bairns this sickly, there had to be more. How many?

———◆———

Gregor spurred his horse forward. "Point in the direction he headed, Nari. I want this bastard."

"That way, my lord!" The lad's excitement at the chase was quite contagious. "We'll catch him. Silver is the fastest horse ever."

"Aye, he is pretty fast." He wouldn't stop until he caught up with Earc. If they caught him now, they'd find Linet more quickly. None of them knew South Berwick at all.

They rode to the edge of town and then beyond it, into a meadow. It wasn't long before he saw the lines of what appeared to be a horse in front of them…a horse that suddenly sped up.

They had the bastard.

Gregor leaned down to Nari, who looked up at him

with shining eyes. "Lad, I'm going to pull abreast of his horse, then jump onto it to knock him off. I don't want to kill him. You'll have to grab the reins when we're close, then calm Silver. Can you do that for me?"

"Aye, I'll do it. Silver likes me," he said, his hands reaching for the reins.

"Not yet. I have to get him close enough to jump. You'll have to wait until I leap."

"I can do it. You can count on me. There he is! We're gaining on him."

"Aye, we are."

Gregor waited until they were alongside Earc, who had tried to change his direction when he had not managed to outpace them. As soon as he was close enough, he said, "Grab the reins, Nari."

He jumped straight at Earc, knocking him off the side of his horse. He sailed across the meadow with him, landing directly on top of him.

In a perfect position for pummeling.

Pummel the bastard he did. When he saw his face was bloodied enough, he paused and grabbed him by his tunic. "Rotten bastard. You dared to defile a Ramsay plaid? You'll lead me to where they're keeping Linet or else."

Earc smirked. "Or else what?"

"Or else I'll take you back and let my brother and Uncle Logan at you at the same time."

Earc dared to chuckle. "Our men did a good job on your Uncle Logan. He's no threat any longer." Earc spat a stream of red saliva off to the side.

Gregor held his dagger at Earc's throat. "And where are all those men you sent after my uncle? How many of them have joined you here? Och, you've forgotten, have you? I'll remind you. They're all dead and my uncle lives. They're as dead as you'll be if you don't lead me to Linet."

A group of horses came up behind him, just as Nari returned with Silver. Gavin, Merewen, Maggie, and Will surrounded him with the other Ramsay guards they'd brought along, some cursing Earc out.

Gavin grinned. "Need some assistance, Gregor? I'd love to help you beat this traitor until he cannot speak."

"Nay, not now. He'll lead us straight to the compound where they're keeping Linet and the other prisoners. Mayhap we'll meet up with our other cousins. You know the Grants, aye, Earc? Connor, Braden, and Roddy Grant are already in South Berwick with a few of their own guards."

Earc's gaze narrowed. "I'll lead you to Linet because I'm outnumbered, but all the Grant and Ramsay guards you have won't be worth anything against the guards the Dubh men have hired. You'll all be killed, so I'm taking you to your death. But 'twill make entertainment for me, so please…allow me to gain my horse and I'll take you straight into the Channel of Dubh." A wicked grin twisted his lips. "You'll see what makes us so powerful. And you'll wish you hadn't."

CHAPTER NINETEEN

LINET SAT IN THE MIDDLE of the small building on a stool, one laddie on her lap. The poor boy could barely lift his head, but she fed him with tiny sips of broth. He awakened whenever the liquid rolled into his wee mouth, and he would swallow and open his eyes to gaze at her.

What an awful situation for these bairns.

She'd fed each one as much as they would take, so she stood up, settled them all, and headed toward the door. "I shall return, Matilda."

The woman said nothing, so she headed back over to the main building. Opening the door as quietly as possible, she peeked around the corner, surprised to see two young lasses cleaning the main hall. No one else was around so she stepped inside. "Greetings to you. Have you seen Sela?"

"Nay," the red-haired lass answered, her nose covered with freckles. She pointed to her friend. "Bess said they took her."

"Who took her?"

Bess blushed and looked away, her tight black plait swinging. "They took her. Dee and Guy. We don't know why. Elsie and I don't ask. We just listen."

"Do you know where they went?"

They shook their heads in tandem.

On a whim, Linet felt compelled to ask, "How old are you lassies?"

Bess replied, "I'm ten summers and Elsie is ten and two."

A sick feeling roiled in her gut, but she thanked them and took an apple from one of the tables. Buffing it on her skirt, she stepped back outside into the gray day. The area they were in was quite deserted, with no clear landmarks nearby and just three buildings in the middle of a forest. Would Gregor ever find her here? How could he?

She found a log at the edge of the clearing and sat down, munching on her apple. Fighting the feeling of hopelessness. Gregor had taught her hope, and she wasn't yet ready to let go of it.

It struck her that something had changed within her. The best evidence she had of this was that she'd had the courage to slap Mal. After years of taking the abuse he heaped on her, accepting his claims that she deserved it and had no choice, she'd stood up for herself. Something she'd never have done when she was younger. And she'd found the strength to open up to Gregor—to let herself fall in love with the only lad who'd ever caught her fancy.

Her love grew for him like the tiniest bud in the spring— tentatively opening, as if afraid to expose itself to the harsh conditions of this world, yet growing stronger every day.

Was there a possibility she could marry one day with her past? She dared to hope so.

This entire chapter in her life had made her stronger. Merewen, Gregor, and even Sela had made her believe she had value in and of herself—that she didn't have to submit to anyone.

And she never would again.

Matilda opened the door and shouted to her. "One of them is crying again." Her face turned to a scowl. "Where did you get that apple? I want it."

Linet looked at the apple in her hand, half-finished, and made a quick decision. If she'd thought any of the sick ones could chew it, she would have brought it to them, but they couldn't at this point. She took a few quick bites of the fleshy fruit, then tossed the core over her shoulder.

She was not sharing with Matilda. The witch yelled, "Selfish," spun on her heel and closed the door.

Mayhap it was time for her to be a little bit selfish, at least toward certain people. She strode over to the small building, opened the door, and reached for the basin of broth.

"You're wasting your time," Matilda sneered. "They'll all die."

Linet arched her brows at the woman. "I see that does not bother you at all."

"Why should I care? They don't belong to me."

Linet was furious at the woman's attitude. How could anyone put such an uncaring beast in charge of bairns? Mayhap it was dangerous to ask questions—she knew who these people were now, and they were indeed dangerous— but she thought it best to get as much information as she could. If she managed to escape, she'd need to know what to tell Gregor and the others.

They had to rescue the bairns.

"Where did they find them? Are there others? If they were in a home for orphans, they must all be sickly. Often times, when one youngster is sick, the others will be, too. At least, 'tis what Mistress Brenna says. And where are Guy and Dee, the two I spoke with earlier? I didn't see them inside just now." True, the lasses inside had told her they'd left, but she wished to hear what Matilda had to say about them. She settled the sleeping laddie back onto his pallet and stood up, smoothing her skirts.

"I don't know where they're from, but I saw them leave," Matilda said.

"Where did they go?"

"They have another place closer to the port. 'Tis much larger than this one. I heard them say there was trouble there."

Linet's gut clenched. This was the confirmation she'd feared. "Do they plan to sell these bairns?"

"How would I know? And why would I care? When the sennight ends, I'll collect my coin and go on my way. I don't wish to know anything. And I would advise you to do the same. Those men are ruthless."

"They're also English."

"Aye, but what does that matter? We're in Scotland now. And since it's the Borderlands, it could all change on the morrow. You know how the Scots and English fight here. But they aren't involved in that. However, you must tread carefully, Miss Lassie who-thinks-she's-better than-me. You'll get yourself in a heap of trouble asking so many questions."

Trouble was something she didn't need. But she couldn't give up. It struck her that Mal was inside and he was the one person who could give her the information the Ramsays needed. "I'm going to get something to eat. Would you like anything?"

"A fruit tart. Tell Cook I want one."

Linet had made it halfway to the main building when the door opened, several guards exiting. Two made crude remarks to her, but she ignored them, intent on her quest. Mal was not with them so he was likely still inside.

She stepped inside the hall, waiting for her eyes to adjust to the darkness before she moved. Mal was seated at the trestle table, eating porridge and bread.

"Miss me already, my sweet?" He chuckled, one of the worst sounds she'd heard in a long time.

"I'm still in shock that my own brother has been involved in such a dreadful operation. How do you sleep at night?" She approached cautiously, making sure she stayed out of reach.

"Verra well. 'Tis all the coin I've gained that keeps me happy."

"Where did the two men in charge go?" she asked as casually as possible.

"They're off to the big building to fetch the rest of the

cargo," he said, licking his fingers after eating a hunk of bread. "We're about to ship off the largest group yet," he said, smacking his lips with a sick sense of pride.

Linet desperately wanted to tell him what she thought of him, but forced herself to focus on gaining information. "And when will the others arrive?"

"Over the next few days."

"Where did you find a ship large enough for that many?"

"It will take three ships. I'll earn enough coin to take you far, far away from Clan Ramsay, the Highlands, and the dreadful gray skies. I hear there are places where the sun shines nearly every day. Just a ship voyage away. Or mayhap I'll find us a place in London. I have not made up my mind yet. Where would you like to live, dear sister?"

She gave him the most scathing look she could muster, although her muscles twitched with the need to run from him. "Nowhere with you. Wherever you take me, I'll find a way to escape."

He bolted out of his chair so quickly it startled her. Grabbing her by the wrist, he pulled her toward the door. "I don't know who gave you the idea you could be such a bitch, but I'll teach you who's in charge."

———

It was near the end of the day when they arrived outside the place where Earc had said they'd find Linet. He held his tied hands up to get their attention. "It's in a clearing up ahead."

"And this is where Linet is being kept?" Gregor asked, yanking him down from his horse and holding a dagger to his throat.

"She should be in there. 'Tis the only place I'm aware of."

"I'll check it out with my falcons," Will said at once. "I'll be right back." Tall and lanky, Will wore the dark clothes they all favored for Band of Cousins activities. His hair was even darker. Of them all, Will knew the most about traveling undetected. He'd lived in a cave for many years, training his two falcons to respond to his voice commands. They could be very effective in scaring or startling someone who was planning unsavory deeds.

They found a place to water their horses, so Gregor suspected the buildings were indeed close by. Every residence needed a water source and this small burn would serve them well. "What else do you know?"

Earc shrugged with a smirk. "Not much. I've only been here once. There are three buildings. Only one large enough to hold many people. In the main building, there's a hall, kitchens, and a chamber to sleep about a dozen."

Maggie turned to Gregor. "This cannot be the center of their operation. 'Tis too small."

"But Linet could be here, could she not?" Merewen's hopeful gaze reminded Gregor he wasn't the only one who had a personal stake in finding Linet. Merewen paced in a small circle, taking in all her surroundings as if searching for her best friend.

Suddenly her eyes widened.

"What is it?" Gavin asked, moving to her side and rubbing her back. "Are you all right?"

"She's here." The expression on her face changed from doubt to elation.

"Where?" Gregor asked, his gaze scanning the area round them.

"I cannot see her, but 'tis as I told you before. I can feel Linet when she's close. but I know she's here." She clasped Gavin's hand and squeezed it. "*She's here.*"

Gavin turned to the others. "I can't explain it either, but I can attest to it. If Merewen says her sister is here, believe it."

Maggie nodded once, decisively. "I wonder if Connor and the others are nearby."

Will returned, his falcons circling overhead. "There is

activity here," he said, his mouth in a flat line. "I hate to say this, but I can hear bairns crying. Three buildings as he said, arranged in a triangle. The crying is coming from the small building farthest from us."

"Did you see any evidence of Connor's group?" Maggie asked.

"Nay. I only saw a few guards at posts. Maybe half a dozen. But the back is all trees, and the one building in back could house quite a few people."

"Did you see Sela?" Gavin asked. "The tall blonde Norsewoman?"

Will shook his head.

"Find Sela, you'll find Connor."

Maggie thought for a moment. "We cannot risk an attack. I don't think this is the main source, and if we kill all who are here, we may never know where the other prisoners are being kept."

"So what do you propose?" Gregor asked, giving Earc a shove so that he fell to the ground, unable to move quickly because he was still restrained.

"We number a dozen with more Ramsay guards on the way. I think you and Gavin should approach the building, ask for Linet. We'll watch and provide cover. Merewen, I know you'd like to go, but I'd prefer having you in the trees with me in case something goes wrong. We don't have the numbers we need, so we must depend on our archers rather than man-to-man fighting."

"But I know she's here," Merewen repeated, emphatic.

Maggie patted her arm. "I know, but if Will heard crying bairns, we must be careful in our approach."

Will said, "I think I should go with Gavin and Gregor. You ladies wait in the trees and be ready to fire arrows if necessary. We'll hold the guards back a bit but let them see we have them with us."

"I think that's our best plan under the circumstances," Maggie agreed. "I'd hoped to find the Grants here."

Gregor bound Earc to a tree, ensuring he was gagged. Maggie pointed to a couple of trees hidden behind a row of pines. This time of year, it was hard to hide in the kind of trees that had lost their leaves. Once Maggie was up in the tree, Will asked, "Can you see well enough?"

Maggie nodded. "I can see all three buildings."

Gavin helped Merewen into a good spot, too, and the three men stepped into the clearing, heading toward the building with the crying bairns. They'd left their guards in the periphery, scattered around them as a show of strength.

To their surprise, a man stepped out of the largest building, dragging a woman who looked just like Linet, though her face was partially hidden. They couldn't hear his words, but he was clearly berating the woman. He swung his arm out and slapped her.

Gregor, a man who prided himself on his calm exterior and ability to control his emotions, lost all his ability to reason in an instant and headed off toward them at a dead run.

The man who'd hit her was Mal.

And Gregor was going to kill him.

CHAPTER TWENTY

GREGOR CAUGHT HIM BY COMPLETE surprise, but he wasn't fast enough to stop the bastard from letting out a shrill whistle that clearly served as a call to action for his men. At least a score of men appeared from behind the building, inside it, even some out of the surrounding forest. When he finally got a look at all of them, it was far more than he had expected.

He didn't care. He hauled his fist back and punched Mal in the face, snapping his head back and felling him to the ground.

"You bastard. How dare you touch your own sister."

Mal grinned as he jumped to his feet and drew his sword, so Gregor did the same.

"Fine, I'm happy to cut your heart out while she's watching."

Linet backed up, eyes wide, but she began to cry as soon as the two swords began to clash. She glanced overhead at the arrows sluicing by, finding their targets.

"Linet, get down or you might get hit," Gregor shouted at her.

The men from Clan Ramsay were far better fighters than the Channel's hired soldiers of fortune. Gavin fell in beside Gregor, quickly slaying two of Mal's men, one on either side of him. Will whistled for his birds and they swooped down several times into the faces of the Dubh men.

Gregor continued to fight, anger driving his sword faster

and harder, but something bothered him.

Linet.

Her hands gripped her hair and she began to wail, her gaze locked on the fight between him and her brother. Her abuser. She began to whirl in a circle, looking at the bodies going down all around her, and her wail changed to a strange sound he didn't comprehend.

He recalled Merewen had acted similarly after her first battle.

But hadn't Linet witnessed the battle at Inverness?

"Linet, stay still or you could be a target." He swung his sword again, blocking a blow meant for his belly. The two parried and fought, the grunts and growls joining the cacophony of battle around them. Still, Linet kept pacing, as if eager to do something although she knew not what. Hellfire, if he couldn't tell Mal was trained as a Ramsay guard. He fought better than all the others.

Merewen called down, "Linet, keep still. I'm afraid I'll hit you."

"Winnie, is that you? Where are you?"

"Don't call to her or the Dubh men will know where she is. She has to stay hidden." He delivered a hard swing to the side, knocking Mal's sword from his hands and leaving him with naught but a small dagger. The noise around them was slowing down, but he couldn't take his gaze from Mal or it could mean his death.

One more blow, and Gregor knocked Mal to the ground. He wanted to kill him—he'd never wanted to kill a man more—but Linet deserved the right to deliver the killing blow to her abuser.

"Linet, take the dagger out of my boot and drive it into his heart. He needs to pay. You deserve justice for what he's done."

Merewen called from the trees, "Mal?"

Linet sobbed and shook her head. Kill her own brother in front of her sister? "Nay, please don't. He's my brother.

Don't kill him. Can we not imprison him? Winnie doesn't know, she'll never understand…"

Mal took that moment and used it against Gregor. "Did you forget I'm from Clan Ramsay? I deserve the right to be tried for my crimes by the Ramsay chieftain, not you. Merewen! Talk sense into this daft man. He's trying to kill me!"

The skirmish had ended and the others gathered around him, questioning looks on their faces. He hadn't told anyone about Mal's abusive treatment of his sister. If he slayed the man now, there'd be questions Linet would not want him to answer.

Merewen cried out, "'Tis truly you, Mal? You're helping the Dubh men?"

She wouldn't have recognized him from her perch in the tree.

"Just for the coin," he whined. "I would have returned to Clan Ramsay in a sennight, after the shipment goes out. Think of my sire and mother," he added, staring at Gregor, "how will they feel if you kill me?"

Gregor could see the gleam in the arse's gaze. He knew he was gaining sympathy from the others, but he could not betray Linet.

Maggie shot Gregor a puzzled look. "Do you know something we don't? He can stand before Uncle Quade, Torrian, and my sire. He'll pay for his involvement. We can hang him in front of our whole clan for his deeds if 'tis our chieftain's judgement."

Gregor glanced at Linet, who was still shaking her head. When she caught his gaze, she reached over to grasp his sword hand. "Gregor, I could not live with myself if you killed him because…"

"After all he's done to you? He's the reason you're here. He had you kidnapped, and what about all the years before this?" Gregor's teeth pained him because he gritted them so hard. If he bit any harder, he'd draw blood. "He deserves to die. Don't ask me to let him go."

Merewen looked back and forth between them. Something in her face crumpled. "Linet, what is he talking about? What about the years before? What didn't you tell me?" Tears slid down her cheeks.

Linet lowered her voice and brought her lips to Gregor's ear. "Please, Gregor. Not here. Keep my secret. Give me more time to tell her."

Gregor glanced at the evil blackheart with the wide grin on his face. He turned to two of the Ramsay guards and said. "Tie him up against that tree over there." They did as he asked and dragged Mal to the side of the clearing.

The others left Linet and Gregor to themselves, but he didn't know what to say to her. So he didn't say anything. He opened his arms and she fell into them. He inhaled her sweetness and reveled in the softness of her curves as she leaned into him, wrapping her arms around his neck and sobbing so hard he wondered how she could have that many tears inside of her.

Out of the corner of his eye, he caught sight of something—Earc.

Someone had freed him, or he'd managed to break his bonds himself, and he rushed straight at them, his sword over his head with the aim to kill.

Gregor pushed Linet away, stepped in front of her, and grabbed and threw his dagger, hitting Earc between the eyes.

As soon as the man crumpled to the ground, dead, Linet let out another scream that rang out over the clearing. What exactly was going on in her mind?

———◆———

Linet ran and ran, not knowing where she was going, just knowing she had to get away—away from the death and blood and killing and screaming...

How had all of this happened?

Then, just when she thought she couldn't take it anymore, any of it, Merewen called out to her. "Linet, please wait. I missed you. We need to stay together. I can't bear to be apart from you any longer."

Linet stopped abruptly and turned around to face her dear sister, then ran to hug her, wrapping her arms so tightly around her that Merewen had to say, "Just let up a bit. I'm still a wee bit sore from last week."

Horrified, she let go but then smiled because Winnie had that same expression she'd always loved. Sheepish and giggly at the same time. "Oh, Winnie, I'm so glad to see you again."

It felt as if a missing piece inside of her had suddenly been restored, as if the world were sane again, or nearly there. Merewen took her wrist and pointed to a large rock. "Please, Linet. We need some time alone. I think there's something you need to tell me."

They were in a corner of the clearing, in a place where they could both see Mal. Linet decided she didn't wish to see his face so she repositioned herself to give him her back.

Reaching for her sister, she hugged her more gently, careful not to hurt her. "I forgot to congratulate on your marriage. I'm so happy for you. You and Gavin are perfect for each other." She paused, then added, "I think I'm in love with Gregor, but he'd never marry someone like me."

Merewen held her finger up to her sister's lips. "Stop right there. I want to discuss this with you, but there is a more pressing matter at the moment. I need to know about Mal. Why does Gregor hate him so? What happened that I don't know about?"

Linet closed her eyes and reached for her sister's hands, clutching them as if they were a rope in the deep sea. She needed to finish what she'd started the night she was stolen from her bed. She needed to tell Merewen the truth. Mayhap it would help her understand Gregor's actions.

"Mal misused me. It started when I was ten and two and lasted a long time."

"Oh, Linet." Tears welled in Merewen's eyes, but they weren't tears of pity. Empathy was the most powerful skill her sister possessed.

"I don't wish to speak of it, but just know that I told Gregor the truth after he rescued me from that awful place. He was so accepting that I thought he could possibly be someone I could love, that maybe you and I were meant to marry cousins, not brothers."

"I'm so sorry, but why did you stop Gregor from killing Mal? He abused you, he's the reason you were kidnapped, *and* he's involved with the Channel. He deserves death. I know he's our brother, but he's never been exceedingly nice to you, only when he called you... Oh Linet."

"Aye, he would call me special, would he not?"

Her sister's eyes turned fiery with rage. "Oh, I'll kill the bastard myself. Don't judge Gregor for doing what Mal deserves. If you don't wish to do it, I'd be happy to kill him for you."

"Nay, let the Ramsays decide what's to happen to him. I hate him, but I didn't want to be the cause of his death. Do you understand?"

"Nay, I don't. You wouldn't be the cause. He's the one who made the mistakes, who..." Merewen glanced over Linet's shoulder at a young girl who appeared to be sneaking over to Mal. The lass's gaze was on the group of warriors, who paid Mal no mind at the moment. "Who is that?"

Linet turned around to look. "Her name is Elsie. She's nice. She was one of the maids in the manor home. She's only two and ten summers, and she has a friend named Bess. Poor lass is probably frightened by what happened. We should reassure her that she won't be hurt."

They both gasped in shock as Elsie stepped behind the tree. She appeared to be doing her best to untie the brute.

Linet glanced over to see if Gregor had noticed, but the cousins were in a heated discussion. Before she could call the situation to their attention, she saw Mal give Elsie a long, lingering kiss on the cheek.

Nay. Nay. Nay. She'd never allow Mal to trick another lass into doing something she didn't wish to do. She'd never let him steal another lass's innocence. She wouldn't allow it.

Linet stood up, glanced at her sister, and declared, "You were right and I was wrong. I'm done being soft-hearted." Her voice erupted in a roar as she clenched her fists and tore across the clearing, headed straight for Mal. "Elsie, run. Stay away from him. As far away as you can!"

Elsie, shocked, stood up and ran, not waiting to see why Linet was so angry.

When Linet reached Mal, she swung her fists at every part of him she could reach.

"I hate you, I hate you! Leave her be. You have no right to touch her or me. Go away and never come back." She kicked him twice, but then something happened she hadn't expected.

Mal grabbed her, swinging her around and holding her in front of him. Elsie had managed to untie him enough for him to free himself. "Don't you ever touch me again," he said, his vile breath in her ear.

Linet bit his forearm and he howled. "You bitch."

Then he made his biggest mistake.

He punched her in the jaw.

CHAPTER TWENTY-ONE

GREGOR BELLOWED, "STAND BACK, LINET."
She did as he said and stepped to the side, giving him enough of an opening to do what he needed to do. Mal reached for her again, but he was too slow.

One arrow struck him in the chest and two in his belly. He fell straight back, his gaze still on Linet.

Gregor raced to her, though she hadn't moved. She just stood there and stared at Mal. The three arrow wounds would kill the bastard, but Gregor wanted to get her away from him. He'd realized the mistake he'd made earlier and didn't intend to repeat it—whatever the arse had done, Linet wouldn't want the memory of watching the life leave her brother's eyes.

He was nearly upon them when Mal picked up his head and said to Linet, "Do not worry. I'll survive this and find myself another one."

Linet leaped on him then, grabbing the arrow in his chest and twisting it. "Nay, nay, nay…"

By the time Gregor wrapped his arms around her to lift her away from him, the light had indeed left Mal's eyes, and they turned up, staring blankly at the trees above them.

Linet turned around and leapt into his arms, launching herself at him with such power that her feet left the ground. She buried her face in his shoulder, wrapped her arms around him so tightly that he couldn't take a deep breath, and sobbed.

Merewen and Gavin came up behind him. "Linet, did he hurt you?"

She picked her head up, her face red and streaked with tears, and barely got out, "Nay. My thanks for protecting me. You shot at him three times, Gregor. Three times and he didn't die. That shows what an evil man he was."

"I didn't fire three arrows," Gregor said, brushing wild hairs away from her beautiful face. "I fired one." He glanced at his cousin, wondering who had shot the other two.

Gavin said, "I hit him once."

Merewen clasped her sister's shoulder. "I hit him once, too. Linet, he deserved to die. His evil heart took over. You mustn't feel badly because I don't."

Linet pulled away from him enough to set her feet back on the ground and looked at all the people around them. The look on her face made him want to take her far, far away from here.

Perhaps that was exactly what she needed.

Another guard yelled, and Maggie approached them at a run. "We have another score of Ramsay guards nearly here, but there is also a group of unidentified horses coming this way. It could be more Dubh men or it could be the Grants. We can't tell. I sent two guards out to find out exactly who they are."

Will strode over and said, "I just had an interesting conversation with one of the Channel guards."

"How did you convince him to talk?" Gavin asked.

"My peregrine sat on his chest for a wee bit. Amazing how fast they talk when staring at the beak of a falcon." His eyes glimmered with satisfaction.

"Finish the tale, husband," Maggie said with a smirk.

"There are two men in charge, and they left a while ago for a larger building where they're keeping more lasses. Next to the port and not far from the castle. The shipment is scheduled to leave in a sennight. Or shipments, I should say. There are many more coming and at least three ships.

Apparently, the two men have connections because they're using Berwick Castle for themselves, though they're not so bold as to keep any prisoners there."

"Interesting…" said Maggie.

"There's more. They left because there is trouble at the other compound."

Gregor's face lit up. "Connor and our Grant cousins."

"Verra possible," Will said.

"I'd say highly probable," said Gavin, who then glared at Gregor and tipped his head toward Linet. She stood with her head on Gregor's shoulder, her gaze fixed on the carnage on the ground.

Maggie whispered, "Why don't you take Linet away from here? With the other guards, we can handle everything."

Gregor glanced at Linet to gauge her reaction, and to his surprise, she gave him a quick nod and whispered, "Please?"

The look in her eyes told him that she was finally beginning to heal—and it promised of a future that he desperately wanted with her.

"Go to Drummond land," Maggie said. "I was going to send a messenger asking for assistance. I think this is going to be more than we can handle. Tell Daniel and David we need them and ask for a score or two of Drummond guards, whatever they can spare."

Merewen hurried into the front house while Linet pointed to the small hut and said, "The bairns in there are ill. Promise you'll protect them? You're right, I cannot handle any more of this chaos. Please, just one day away? Then we'll return to help."

Maggie reached for her hand and squeezed it. "We'll take care of the bairns. I've already sent Matilda on her way. She was a miserable one, was she not?"

Linet nodded. "She was indeed. I'm glad she's gone."

Merewen returned with a sack and said, "Here, these looked like your things. Go to Drummond land. They say 'tis beautiful."

The sisters hugged, and Linet said, "I love you, Winnie."

Gavin brought Silver to them, Nari riding him. "What about me?"

"We still need you here, Nari," Maggie said, "if you'll stay and help."

"Aye!" he said, perking up. He hopped off the back of the horse. "I can't wait to tell Thorn about all I've done to help."

Gregor lifted Linet onto his horse, then tied the sack to his saddle and mounted.

Maggie held a hand up and said, "Good work. We've saved another group of lasses and lads. Now go before any more men arrive." She slapped the horse's flank and they were off.

———◆———

Linet leaned back against Gregor, closing her eyes for a bit just because she'd cried so hard they were sore. She couldn't cry any more tears.

Some of her tears were for the atrocities she'd seen—dead men, sick bairns, Dubh men. But some of her tears were grateful, happy tears.

She was truly free. Mal would never bother her again.

She rested her head against Gregor's shoulder, staring at the darkness of the forests and the glens they passed. One thing was for certain, despite all she'd seen and done, despite all that had been done to her, she had no fears at the moment.

Why? Because she knew Gregor would protect her.

Now that she was away from the chaos, she focused on the man who held her. She trusted him more than any man she knew. That was something she couldn't ignore.

He rubbed her forearm and kissed the back of her neck. "Sweetings, I think we'll need to stop for the night. I don't know this land as well as my own. I'm going to listen for water and search out an area hidden from the main path."

Half an hour later, they heard the sound of rushing water. They couldn't see the falls, but they followed it by ear.

A light snow had fallen and the moon reflected off the white on the ground, lighting the way for them.

"You are not worried about being followed, are you, Gregor?"

"Nay," he said, turning their horse toward the waterfall. "No one in this area is interested in us. Besides, if the shipment meant to go in a sennight is as large as they say, every reiver and renegade in Scotland and England will be in South Berwick looking to gain coin."

The closer they came to the waterfall, the louder it became. When it finally came into view, Linet smiled. It was the most beautiful waterfall she'd ever seen. It was twice the height of any man, and the water fell into a small pool at the base, where a row of small pines grew as if planted there for protection against the cold Highland wind.

Gregor dismounted and said, "Allow me to check the area. I think I might see a cave behind the waterfall."

Linet sighed. That sounded so lovely. The first twenty years of her life, she'd rarely traveled from Ramsay land. In the past moon or so, she'd seen much more than any of her friends in Clan Ramsay. Inverness, Edinburgh, South Berwick, and now they were away to Drummond land in Crieff.

Gregor returned and reached for her waist to help her down. "We're in luck. This cave is not so large as the last one, but 'twill protect us from the elements. It goes in deep enough to keep us from getting wet from the waterfall." Once he had helped her down, he reached for her sack and his saddlebag, then took her hand to lead her back to the cave.

She giggled when the cold water splashed her a bit as they entered the cave, but it refreshed her enough that she thought she'd take a bold step. Once they were inside, she opened her sack to see what Winnie had packed for her, surprised to see how thorough her dear sister had been. She'd packed an extra gown, wool leggings, a good sized linen square, plus a loaf of bread and some cheese. "Oh my, this bread is fresh from the oven. The cook must have just baked it."

"I'm glad your sister packed it. Those men won't benefit from her cooking any longer."

"Merewen must have found my little stash. This sliver of soap was next to my bed."

Gregor grinned. "Lavender," he said, leaning down to take in the aroma. His gaze caught on something else inside the sack. He reached inside and asked, "May I?"

Linet nodded, willing to share anything with this man. "Aye, What is it?"

He reached inside and pulled out the gift he'd made her many years ago. "You kept this?"

"Of course."

He pulled it out, running his hand over the fine wood grain he had sanded into a soft sheen. He kissed her cheek and said, "I'll have to find a new book for you."

"My apologies, Gregor, but my sire destroyed the one you gave me."

"Fear not, I'll find you more and you'll never have to hide your love of reading again."

She kissed him on the lips, running her fingers through his thick, wavy locks, wondering how she'd ever been so fortunate as to have found this man. Her gaze turned and stared out at the water as it fell over the outcropping, at a perfect angle for her to wash her hair and body. How she wished it were summer so she could stand underneath the water, relish in its freshness, and feel clean.

After all she'd been through of late, she couldn't help but feel dirty.

Gregor wrapped his arm around her waist and nuzzled

her neck. "If I make a fire in the corner there and go out hunting so you can have your privacy, will you do it?"

She spun around, a wide smile on his face because he'd known exactly what she was thinking. "How did you…"

"The look of longing on your face as you stared at the water, holding the soap firmly in your hand. I'll promise not to look if you wish. It's likely too cold for you to want to stay in it for long. I might even take a plunge myself once you're done. As long as I can keep a fire going, I think it's a luxury we should enjoy. It is at the perfect height for both of us."

She let him see her eagerness. For far too long, she'd hidden how she felt, but that was something she'd rather not do with Gregor. "I would love to try it, but only if you can get a fire going."

He gave her a quick kiss on the lips and said, "I'll go find some wood and brush to get it started."

A short time later, he returned and started the fire on the far side of the cave, at the edge of the waterfall. The water missed that corner, so she hoped it would stay lit.

"I'll see what else I can find to eat," Gregor said.

Linet settled her hands on her hips, looking at the cascading water not far from her. She had to know. What would it be like to be with Gregor? To feel his skin against hers, his heat pressed against her flesh, his lips on her body.

"What is it?" he asked.

She reached to the back of her hair and pulled the ties out, unplaiting her dark locks and allowing them to fan over her shoulder. Then she tugged at her gown and tossed it off to the side, leaving herself in just her chemise and wool stockings.

She turned to Gregor with her hands folded in front of her in invitation. "Join me, Gregor."

Gregor's expression told her she'd shocked him more than she had thought.

CHAPTER TWENTY-TWO

———◆———

LINET TREMBLED, BUT SHE WOULDN'T change her mind. Not now. If she were ever to be with any man, it would be this man in front of her. Gregor represented everything good in life—honorable, hard-working, honest, compassionate, tender, and intelligent. It didn't hurt that he was the handsomest man she'd ever met.

His eyes, those warm brown eyes, had the ability to make her mind turn to mush whenever he looked at her. Had her regard for him deepened into love? Was *this* what love felt like?

She didn't know, but after nearly losing her life, she didn't wish to wait to find out.

She stepped close enough to touch his face, trailing her fingers down the rough stubble of his jaw. "Gregor, I want you, and I hope you want to be with me. We've known each other a long time, and my feelings for you grow stronger every time we're together. I'm falling in love with you."

He sighed and closed his eyes, tipping his head down so that his forehead touched hers. "You don't know how tempting you are to me, lass. But I cannot lie with you when we're not married. I wish to continue our relationship, but it would not be right. My sire taught me to respect women."

"I am not a maiden. You know my past. No man will want me," she said, a tear sliding down her cheek. "'Tis unlikely I'll ever marry, but I don't want to live my life without knowing what it could be like…with you. I wish to know what it's like with someone I love."

She touched her lips to his, holding his hand, and a low growl ripped from deep inside him. He cupped her face and kissed her deeply, reverently. She marveled at how gentle he was, though his kiss turned more urgent, more demanding. When she parted her lips for him, his tongue swept inside her mouth, causing a tingling sensation to travel all over her body until her nipples strained against the shift she wore.

When he ended the kiss, he said, "I love you, Linet, and I don't care about your past. Come to the waterfall with me?"

She smiled and answered him with one movement, lifting her shift off and removing her wool stockings. "You'll have to keep me warm."

His gaze took in everything, dropping to her breasts and below, a hunger in his gaze that pleased her because she knew she'd incited it. If he always looked at her like that, she would be a lucky woman. A part of her wished to run and hide, but somehow, the trust and the love she saw in his gaze stayed her fear. Gregor loved her as she did him, and this would be a wonderful experience between them. He'd said he wasn't very experienced, and neither was she, so they could learn together.

She vowed to trust him completely.

"Love, I still cannot do this without something more formal between us."

"Formal? What do you mean?"

"Handfast with me. I know of others in my family who have done it, though 'tis not common. Promise me that if we still suit, you'll marry me in a year and a day. If we do not make a good match, we'll go our separate ways."

She had to think about this. She stepped closer, her hand reaching up to touch him, attempting to mimic the tenderness he'd shown her. Her finger trailed a path from the bone underneath his chin over to his nipple, then to the coarse hairs on his chest, hesitating there a bit before she trailed her hand down to his belly and…well, she need not wonder whether Gregor wanted her or not.

She'd thought she'd never marry. Seeing her mother's unhappiness, her brother's cruelty, it had soured her on the very thought. But Gregor was a different sort of man altogether.

"Gregor, I'm not sure if I could ever marry," she said, deciding he deserved her honesty in this. "I know nothing of normal relationships."

He trailed a line of kisses down her jaw, making her stand on her tiptoes because it excited her so. "I pledge to let you go if 'tis what you want then." Pulling away, he lifted her chin so their gazes locked. "We cannot have a physical relationship without handfasting. Those are my terms."

"I accept," she whispered, leaning in for a kiss to seal their bargain.

"I don't know how to formally do this other than to say I pledge myself to you for a year and a day, at which time I agree to set you free if 'tis what you want."

If love could be seen in a mere gaze, she knew exactly what it would look like. Gregor looked at her with such admiration and respect, how could she not wish to see what life would be like with him?

"I pledge myself to you for a year and a day, and I will set you free if 'tis what you want," she whispered, their faces nearly touching. "Until that day, I will consider you my husband."

"And you my wife."

They kissed to seal the agreement, then he reached up to his brooch and dropped his plaid before removing his tunic, boots, and hose. He held his arm out to her. "Are you ready, wife?"

Linet giggled at the term, her nervousness overpowering

her a bit. "Aye, I'm ready. Shall we enter our fine bath?" She held her hand out toward the bubbling pool at the foot of the falls. "You first."

He laughed and stepped ahead of her. "I'll go in first, just to be certain there's a bottom and there are no creatures inside."

She stood off to the side to watch him, pleased by the fine figure he cut. His muscles rippled with each step, even when he stopped under the falls to tip his head back, washing his hair before he swung it wide, sending droplets of water all over her.

Flinching and squealing, she cried, "'Tis cold."

"Nay, 'tis not so bad," he said just before he dunked his body into the pool of water at the base of the cascading water. Water spilled from a layer of rocks at one end of the small pool into the burn that joined the stream in the distance.

He held his hand out to her after he'd swum around the pool. "Come, you can touch easily. You'll be surprised to see 'tis actually warm. There must be a warm spring connected to it."

She put her hand in his and stepped in carefully, not willing to submerge as quickly as he had. The first bite of cold water made her cringe, but she quickly adjusted to the temperature. "You're right." She moved toward him, squealing as she submerged her shoulders into the cool water. "I brought my soap." She held her hand out to show him.

"May I?"

She offered it to him without a second thought, but to her surprise, he made a lather from it and used it on her shoulders, lifting her out of the water and washing her back. She couldn't help but moan from his ministrations, reveling in the now tepid pool, the wondrous feeling of being clean, and having his patient assistance in her bathing efforts.

What more could she ask for?

"Gregor, your touch is wonderful." She tipped her head back and leaned it on his shoulder, enjoying his attentions.

"May I wash your front? Will you allow me to touch your breasts?"

Pleased with the respect he'd shown her, and with the bolt of excitement it shot through her, she spun around to give him a quick kiss. "Aye, and many thanks for asking."

His smile was tentative, and if she were to guess, she'd say he was as nervous about their joining as she was. She returned her head to his shoulder. He lathered his hands with soap again and then washed her front, her breasts just barely out of the water. He massaged carefully and methodically, not missing any crevice as he held each mound up to wash the underside. Tingles shot through her breasts.

"Do you like this?"

"Mmmmm… Aye, verra much. Keep washing." She closed her eyes, hoping her excitement would conquer her fear. Gregor deserved to have a willing wife, and she wanted to enjoy this connection with the man she loved. The more time they spent together, the more she trusted him.

He did as she instructed and continued to wash until he had her wild with a yearning she didn't understand. She stood up and turned to him. "Now?"

He said, "I'll follow you out. Go warm yourself by the fire."

She glanced over her shoulder, noticing he was washing himself. Forcing herself to stop staring at his well-honed body, she huddled near the fire to dry off.

His voice carried over the sound of water to her. "Have you changed your mind? 'Tis your choice. If you'd like to wait, we may."

She chewed on her bottom lip, considering her answer, but she knew, trepidation aside, what her answer would be. It was time for Linet to live her life the way she wished,

and what she wanted was to lie in the arms of Gregor
Ramsay.

———————

Gregor climbed out of the pool because he wished to
see her face. "Do you want this as much as I do?" he asked,
needing to know.

"Aye, I want you, Gregor. I want you as my husband and
my friend, as my protector and my confidante. Whichever
you are, I want you and only you."

He covered her lips with his, trying to convey how
much he loved her. He wasn't quite confident in his ability
to pleasure her, since he had so little experience, but he'd
do his best to let her know how he felt with his actions.
His passion overtook him and he devoured her, angling his
mouth over hers so he could taste every bit of her.

To his surprise, she responded with a powerful passion
of her own, one that fueled his desire. He ended the kiss
and took her hand, leading her to the spot inside the cave
where he had layered plaids and furs, settling them both
down on their sides facing each other.

He decided now was the time to confess. "I'm new at
this, in case I bumble along."

She smiled, her hand reaching up to cup his stubbled
cheeks. "Make no mistake, Gregor. This is as new to me as
'tis to you. This is about us showing the love we have for
one another, something I've never done before."

She'd put voice to his own thoughts, which only convinced him of how perfect they were for each other. He
kissed her again, then lowered his mouth to her breast, taking his time to tease her nipple until it peaked, and suckled
her until she cried out. Her hand clutched his one arm,
her nails digging into his skin whenever he did something
she liked. Not knowing what else to do, he maneuvered
her onto her back, settled himself between her thighs, and
whispered, "Guide me?"

She took him in her hand and teased her entrance until he thought he'd spend himself then and there. "More…"

Spreading her legs, she guided him inside until he thought he could go no farther, but as soon as he began to move, she opened wider, giving him greater access.

She whispered one word to him, and he was glad to oblige her. "Faster."

Leveraging himself on his elbows, he kissed her neck as he found his rhythm. She joined him in her need, her breathing as raspy as his own. She pushed him farther, changing his angle in just the right way to please her, and he followed her lead, pounding into her so desperately that he thought he might hurt her.

"Please, harder."

He did as she asked until he nearly spilled his seed inside her, but he managed to control himself until her breath caught, again and again, and she finally tumbled over the edge, calling his name. He echoed her, doing the same as he hurtled into his own chasm of pleasure, something entirely new to him.

When they finished, he couldn't move, so overwhelmed by their love that all he could do was stare into her eyes.

"I love you, Gregor." Her eyes misted and he kissed her tears away, slowly, tenderly.

"This is not a time to cry, but a time to rejoice that we've found each other again. I love you more than I thought possible, and I'm quite sure it will be forever, not just a year and a day."

CHAPTER TWENTY-THREE

THEY ARRIVED AT DRUMMOND CASTLE when the sun was highest. Linet had to admit she felt as though she had a glow about her—one Gregor Ramsay had put there. His tenderness and loving nature had put a smile on her face and a warm feeling deep in her belly.

Gregor greeted the men who rode out to welcome them, introducing them to her as Daniel and Uncle Micheil. He had told her about his two cousins and about Daniel's missing hand.

"I'm guessing there may be a reason you're here," Daniel said, quirking his head to the side.

"Aye, we'll talk inside. Is David in residence?"

"Aye, we are all here. We've been anxious to hear about the progress of the Band. After the battle at Inverness, I've been anxious to join the next effort, but the last we heard you were all back on Ramsay land."

Drummond Castle was indeed beautiful. The cottages outside the bailey were lined up in neat, orderly rows, and many clansmen came out to greet them. But the castle grounds impressed her most of all. The bushes were neatly trimmed, planted in purposeful groupings, something she'd never seen before. A great pine tree surrounded by smaller bushes sat in each corner of the bailey, and trees in large pots decorated either side of the entrance.

The greenery, even in winter, made the castle warmer, more appealing.

Once inside, a bubbly red-headed lass hurried over to greet them, followed by a beautiful dark-haired woman, whom she guessed to be Gregor's Aunt Diana. She carried herself like a chieftain would.

"Greetings," the red-headed lass said, "my name is Constance and I'm married to Daniel. You must be Linet. I was with your sister in Inverness. We searched everywhere for you. 'Tis so lovely to finally meet you."

She liked Constance immediately. The rest of the introductions were a blur—Anna and David, Lady Drummond, and two others she didn't recall.

Lady Drummond said, "Please sit over by the hearth where you can warm yourself. I'll go to the kitchens and arrange for some food for you. Gregor, do you eat like Gavin? If I recall, you don't, but I'll bring out as much as you would like."

Gregor moved protectively to Linet's side and said, "A light repast is fine. We've much to tell you."

Once they were all settled around a trestle table, Daniel looked Gregor in the eye and said, "Are we any closer?"

"Aye," Gregor replied. "Maggie asked me to send for you and David, plus some additional guards if possible."

Linet added, "While I was being held by the Channel, I found out several things. The main group and holding is in South Berwick and their largest building is near the docks."

Daniel whistled. "That gives them access to the sea. We must stop them."

"I was also told by one of the group's leaders that their largest shipment ever is going soon, that it would require three ships, and the men in charge will pay anything to get this shipment off. He claimed the Ramsays were no longer a threat because he and Earc knew everything there was to know about the Ramsay warriors. The Channel has many more men than Clan Ramsay, according to this man's boasts."

Diana gasped. "More than Clan Ramsay? 'Tis more than any of us have."

It would have frightened Linet to hear her say so, but she and Gregor had already discussed what would happen next.

"Except for Clan Grant," Gregor said. "They have nearly seven hundred warriors. While Uncle Alex would never send them all, Maggie is hoping to meet up with Connor so he can send a request home for at least two hundred Grant warriors—their verra best. We're planning to return to Ramsay land to see what they've heard from the Grants, if anything. Maggie needs to assemble as many guards as possible close to South Berwick."

"Their verra best would be the two lairds and Connor," David said. "Mayhap Loki."

"Plus Braden and Roddy. They're already in South Berwick with Connor."

Diana said, "Micheil and I will speak with the guards, choose our best. And I'll also send someone to Aunt Avelina's."

Gregor said, "I'm sure that would be appreciated."

Uncle Micheil shook his head. "If these Dubh men think they're only going to have to fight the Ramsay men, they have no idea what they are about to go up against. It's not only the Ramsay guards, but the Drummonds, the Menzies, and soon the Camerons and the Grants."

"You forgot something important, Uncle Micheil," Daniel said.

"Oh," he asked, quirking his brow. Linet could tell this family often teased each other, and warmly.

A huge grin lit Gregor's face. "I believe I know where you're going with this, Daniel. The Channel of Dubh is about to meet the entire Band of Cousins all at once."

EPILOGUE

—————

L INET AND GREGOR ARRIVED BACK on Ramsay land the next day. They still had five days until the shipment was due to leave. Gregor was becoming more and more upset about the possibility that he might not make it back in time to assist his cousins.

Linet feared for him, but she knew he'd never forgive himself if he missed the chance to help his cousins extinguish the Channel of Dubh for good. She urged him to go back, but he insisted on introducing her to the clan as his partner. At first, she'd thought not to tell her parents or anyone else the truth about Mal, but Gregor insisted.

"This isn't time to feel sorry for your brother. 'Tis time to set things right. Your parents deserve to know why you chose not to return. They shouldn't mourn your brother as if he were a hero."

"I will talk to them," she said, kneading her hands in the folds of her skirts, doing her best to hide it.

Gregor reached for her hands and said, "I'll go with you."

"You needn't come, Gregor. I'll be fine." But even as she said the words, she doubted they were true. How could she admit to her parents that she'd twisted the arrow in Mal's wicked heart until his last breath had left him?

"You are correct. I don't need to, but I would like to. Come, let's speak to them now. You'll dread this until you do it."

And her heart swelled a bit more for the love of Gregor

Ramsay. She nodded and they headed out the door toward the huts. They walked in silence, Linet focusing on what she would say.

She was so upset that she didn't even recall stepping inside and sitting at the table, her parents greeting them both.

"Mama, we have bad news for you," she whispered. Gregor stood behind her, his hands on her shoulders for support. "Mal…"

"Mal is dead," her sire blurted out. "Struan heard that he was with those Dubh men," he continued, his voice raising with each question. "Is it true? Was he a traitor?"

Gregor nodded, but didn't speak.

Linet said, "Aye, 'tis true he was working with the Dubh men in Edinburgh and Berwick."

Her father began his pacing. "I cannot believe it. How do you know this to be true? He was a good lad, he would never…"

"Papa, he had me tied up and transported to Berwick against my will. He…"

Her mother's sobbing stopped her. "He had a sickness, did he not, Linet? He…" Her voice cracked and her hands came up to her throat.

Linet said, "He was the reason I did not wish to return to Clan Ramsay."

"What are you saying? Finnola? What sickness?" Her father clearly had no idea what her brother had been doing. All she could do was let the tears fall. Looking at the pain in her dear mother's eyes was more than she could bear. She stared at her father instead, and so she saw the exact moment when understanding filled his eyes.

"Linet, did Mal…do you mean he was…he…?" The man fell into a chair by the hearth, his face stark white. "Nay, I don't believe it. I cannot believe it. He was a good lad…"

"A good lad who was in charge of the Channel of Dubh

in Edinburgh?" Gregor asked.

"In charge? But you said he was involved."

"Linet was being kind. He was in charge of that portion of the Channel. He had Linet kidnapped and nearly forced her to work as a whore."

Wallace Baird's eyes widened, and her mother's sobs continued. He looked to Linet again, his expression turning furious.

"He used you, Linet? My daughter? His own sister?" He stared up at the ceiling before whispering, "I'll kill him myself."

"There's no need," Gregor said softly. "He's gone, and he'll not harm your daughter or any other lass again."

Her mother looked at her and uttered one word, a linen square crushed in her hand. "Struan?"

"Nay, Mama." She reached for her mother's hand and squeezed it. "Struan never hurt me, and he knew naught of what happened."

"Merewen?" her mother whispered.

"Nay, he did not touch her."

Her mother reached for her and wrapped her arms around her, sobbing into her shoulder. "I'm so sorry, Linet."

She allowed her mother to cry for a few minutes, but then decided it was time to put an end to her parents' torture. "Mama, I have good news."

Her mother mopped at her tears and sat up straight. "Please do tell."

"Gregor and I are married." She glanced over at her husband, so proud and pleased that she was overwhelmed. Whether handfasted or married didn't matter to her.

Gregor said, "I asked Linet to marry me and she agreed. We are husband and wife."

Her mother jumped to her feet and hugged her. "Praise the Lord for this blessing. You and Merewen will both be staying here. I'm so glad to have you home, lass."

Her father congratulated both of them, his face beaming,

and though the pain had not left his gaze completely, she thought they would both heal.

Gregor placed his hand on the small of her back and said, "We must go speak with my parents, so we'll take our leave."

They said little on the walk to the keep, but Gregor wrapped his arm around her for support.

"Gregor, you must go back and help your cousins. You need not stay with me. Once we've seen your parents and you've checked on the guards, you should head back to South Berwick." She gave him a kiss on the lips, a sultry, provocative one, but then said, "They need you. I do, too, but I can wait."

Her nerves were getting the best of her as they waited in the hall for Gregor's parents to come down. They'd arrived early, before Brenna and Quade had risen. Lily had greeted them with the twins and the two lassies had showered them with their love. Torrian came down next, pleased to see that Linet had been returned safely. Once he heard of the upcoming battle in South Berwick, he left to speak with Kyle about sending more guards with Gregor.

The door opened at the end of the hall and Gregor's parents entered, Quade using his wooden cane for support. Brenna hastened toward them, her face lit with a bright smile. "You've married, Gregor? Is that what I have heard?"

Linet blushed so deeply she feared her face would stay that dark red forever, but fortunately, she was wrong. Gregor kissed his mother's cheek and clasped his sire's shoulder, making sure he didn't topple the man.

"Mama, Papa, Linet and I agreed to handfast. Due to the circumstances, we felt that was best. We weren't quite ready for marriage, and there were no priests around, so 'tis what we decided. I love Linet with all my heart, and I'm proud to bring her to you as my wife—in my eyes."

Mistress Brenna clasped Linet's cheeks and then hugged her, her enthusiasm convincing Linet that she truly was happy with the match.

Quade said, "We welcome you to the family, Linet. Handfasting is akin to marriage in my eyes, so we consider you to be our son's wife. You are one of our clan. We could not be more pleased to accept you as our daughter. Come," he said, gesturing toward the hearth, "let's sit and talk."

They made their way to the hearth, where Gregor positioned his chair next to Linet's and reached for her hand.

Even that wee bit of consideration made Linet sigh. She had chosen a most thoughtful man.

Once they were all settled, Quade glanced at his wife. "I hear Linet was put to work as the healer in the Channel. Mayhap this will fit nicely with what we've discussed of late."

Mistress Brenna stared at her wide-eyed. "You still have an interest in healing, my dear?"

"Aye, 'tis one of the reasons I wished to stay. I enjoyed it and I was needed."

"And the other reason?" Quade asked.

"Papa," Gregor interrupted. "We'll leave that part for another time. She enjoyed teaching the other lasses to read and healing their injuries."

Mistress Brenna's eyes lit up and her smile widened. "How intuitive of you, Quade. She is exactly what we need."

Gregor looked as confused as Linet felt. What could she mean? "Mama?" he whispered.

"Oh, 'tis naught," she said. "I'm perfectly well, only I've been wanting to slow down…"

"Ahem…"

Mistress Brenna smiled at her husband. "Your sire, Gregor, has been after me to slow down. I've been having a few more pains in my back, but we don't have another well-trained healer. I've been trying to decide who we could use, someone young yet not completely inexperienced. I don't know that I will ever be able to completely walk away from my life's purpose, but the time has come to share my knowledge with another."

Gregor asked the same question Linet had been thinking. "Not Jennet?"

Brenna chewed on her lower lip and tipped her head back and forth. "Jennet, well…she's not ready yet. She has the knowledge, and she'll be a wonderful resource for you, if you decide to accept our offer, Linet, but she doesn't have the compassion or the maturity necessary to take over my duties as of yet."

"Offer?" That was the only word Linet could get out because the thought of working next to Mistress Brenna was so exciting that she had to fight the urge to run about the keep and shout her happiness for all to hear.

"'Tis most perfect. Since you've married Gregor, you'll of course be living at the keep with him. We'll find you a larger chamber than the one he sleeps in at present. The clan will readily accept you since they all already know you. 'Tis most perfect."

"Mama?" Gregor nudged.

"Of course, I'm rambling with excitement. Linet, would you like to train with me to become one of our clan's healers?"

Speechless, she glanced at Gregor, who gave her a brief nod. The look in his eyes told her he would support whatever she chose. Of course he would. She'd chosen a rare man. "I don't know…I…of course…I mean to say that naught would please me more. I'd be honored to assist you and learn your skills."

The door banged open and Logan Ramsay strode into the hall, followed by Gavin and Merewen and Nari, who raced straight for Gregor.

"What is it, Nari?"

"We have not found Connor and Thorn yet!" he cried out. "Do you think something happened?"

"Do not worry, lad," Gregor said. "We'll find them." He

ruffled the lad's hair, but Nari clung to him a bit harder, grabbing hold of his tunic sleeve.

"I miss Thorn already. Where could they be? Will you not help us?"

Gregor knelt down to look the lad in the face. "Aye, I will help you. Connor and Thorn are verra resourceful. Don't forget Braden and Roddy are with them, too, so I'm not worried. We'll find them for certes. And we'll stop the bad men for good." He stood up to glance at his parents and Linet. "I better be leaving shortly. This young lad is Nari and he helped me find Linet in Edinburgh. I think we must hurry. As soon as I fill my belly, we'll be leaving." He nodded a greeting to Gavin and Merewen.

Brenna left for the kitchens, presumably to get food.

"Quade," Logan said, "we had a couple of traitors on our hands Earc and Mal, and now those bastards have more men than we do. I've already sent a messenger to the Grants for assistance. I know not how many extra warriors we need, but we have to start calling on our allies. If we manage to stop that last shipment from going out, we might put a stop to this travesty. The two men in charge of the Channel are reportedly in South Berwick. I want those bastards."

Linet asked, "Merewen, are you going with them?"

"Aye," Merewen said. "They have need of archers. Will you be all right if I leave you here?"

"Aye," she said, grasping her sister's hand in hers. "You do what you must do. Gregor and I handfasted, so I'll be staying here in the keep. Mistress Brenna has asked me to train with her, learn more about healing, and I've accepted. Do me a favor, please. There was a lass named Alys who was verra nice to me. I don't know what happened to her." She described her to Merewen as best she could, hoping the lass could be located and helped.

Merewen's face lit up and she leaned in to hug Linet. "I'll do my best to find her. I'm so happy for you. Are you sure you'll be okay if we go?"

"Aye," she said, choking up at the memories that popped into her mind. "I was there, so I know how important 'tis to stop them."

The hall quieted around her, all eyes now on her.

She couldn't stop the quivering of her chin, but she spoke anyway. "I was with five of the kidnapped bairns. They are starving them. I tried to feed them broth and they could barely take it. I was quite sure at least one of them would die. You must hurry. There's a larger group of bairns they're keeping closer to the docks."

"You've met the men in charge of this operation?" Uncle Logan asked.

"Aye, they are cold and ruthless. They are both English, but 'tis all I can tell you. They were there for a short time, but they returned to the location near the docks. One is known as Dee and the other is Guy, though those are not their real names. Matilda said she'd been hired just to watch bairns for seven days. I think there are many, many more. So many that I know not how you'll handle them all once you locate them."

"Can you think of anything else you learned?" Logan asked, his piercing green eyes boring through her.

"They left before Gregor and Gavin arrived, headed to the Channel's larger establishment near the port, because they were advised of trouble there. They've more bairns there."

"Connor, mayhap?" Gavin's eyes lit up with an expression she could only describe as hope.

"Possibly. They never said. Mal said they were hiring three ships to take the cargo. There are so many lasses and lads coming in over the next few days, even he did not know the number. But I know you must not tarry. If you do, my guess is that hundreds of them will be sent across the waters."

Guy and Dee stood inside a small room arguing.

"I can't believe the bastards took out more of our men and got the bairns," Guy ground out, clenching his teeth as he finished.

Dee cast an expression of derision at him. "Our sickest bairns. They probably would not have survived the boat."

"But they killed another dozen of our men."

Dee waved off his concerns. "So we lost a dozen? We have nearly two hundred men at this point, fifty with us and one hundred and fifty English knights to arrive when we signal our need. And the bairns were a small fraction of our shipment. The older ones are much heartier. Do not worry. The knights will be on the front line, and those wild savages will not be able to take down our chain-mailed warriors. They are the best in all of England."

"If we can keep our true cargo hidden. If the knights find out what they fight for, half of them could desert us. Curse them, we don't need those savage Highlanders interfering at this point."

Dee was not to be swayed. "Those knights care little as long as they get their coin. Cease your worry. Once we've moved all of this shipment out, I'm taking a group out after that Band. We'll get rid of the lot of them."

Guy smirked. "Why stop with the cousins? I say go after all the Ramsays and the Camerons. Then we can liberate the coffers of Lochluin Abbey."

Dee thought for a moment before he nodded. "You may have a point. The Band, then the Ramsays." His eyes narrowed. "But I want that bitch, Maggie Ramsay. I'll enjoy killing her."

DEAR READER,

Thank you for reading Gregor's story. The reason it is shorter than usual is because it is actually taking place in the same time frame as some of Connor's novel. It became difficult for me to separate the two.

Connor's novel has been percolating in my head ever since Gavin's story. Once his story solidified in my mind, it was all I could do to finish Gavin and Gregor's stories first. Connor's story will be everything you'd hoped for and more.

Happy reading!

Keira Montclair

www.keiramontclair.com
www.facebook.com/KeiraMontclair
www.pinterest.com/KeiraMontclair

ABOUT THE AUTHOR

Keira Montclair is the pen name of an author who lives in Florida with her husband. She loves to write fast-paced, emotional romance, especially with children as secondary characters in her stories.

She has worked as a registered nurse in pediatrics and recovery room nursing. Teaching is another of her loves, and she has taught both high school mathematics and practical nursing.

Now she loves to spend her time writing, but there isn't enough time to write everything she wants! Her Highlander Clan Grant series, comprising of eight standalone novels, is a reader favorite. Her third series, The Highland Clan, set twenty years after the Clan Grant series, focuses on the Grant/Ramsay descendants. She also has a contemporary series set in The Finger Lakes of Western New York and a paranormal historical series, The Soulmate Chronicles.

Her latest series, The Band of Cousins, stems from The Highland Clan but is a stand-alone series.

Contact her through her website, *www.keiramontclair.com*.